More books by Greg Cornwell

Twilight – A defence of death with dignity

The John Order Series:

Order and the Suspect Suicide

Order and Mrs Cohen's Conviction

Order and the Abandoned Body

Order and the Merimbula Mystery

Order and the Luckless Lovers

Order and the Parliamentary Conference

Order and the Motel Murder

Order and the Curse Crime

JOHN ORDER POLITICIAN & SLEUTH SERIES BOOK 1

GREG CORNWELL

ORDER
AND THE
SUSPECT SUICIDE

Copyright © 2021 Greg Cornwell

ISBN: 978-1-922565-03-7
Published by Vivid Publishing
A division of Fontaine Publishing Group
P.O. Box 948, Fremantle
Western Australia 6959
www.vividpublishing.com.au

Cataloguing-in-Publication data is held at the National Library of Australia.

To a patient Meg

ONE

"**D**on't."

The rifle briefly rose and John Order, a Member of Parliament of the Australian Capital Territory legislature, settled back in the chair.

Three months after the by-election and with a majority of 176 votes - a figure forever at the forefront of his mind as he carried out his daily duties - Order needed no encouragement from the Party secretary to get out and door knock the electorate.

This was why he found himself sitting in the lounge-room of a rundown Canberra guvvie, a clipboard across his knees, facing an armed man and his nose tingling from stale cigarette smoke.

"You said you wanted to talk," he began, remembering their initial meeting at the front door.

Whatever you do don't go inside, Bernie had cautioned, you'll waste too much time. A quick smiling introduction, hand over a business card and then away, unless someone had a question or a problem to be noted on the clipboard.

Fat chance faced with a rifle.

"Yes. But it's complicated." He was well spoken.

Tall and lean, like Order himself, but with long mousy hair rather than the dark crop on his own head. The man looked morose and tired.

"Howso?"

"You wouldn't understand. I don't even know why you're here."

he added, emphasising the situation with another jerk of the weapon.

"You said you were from Sydney. Been here long?" He'd already explained his visit.

"Couple of weeks."

"Looking for a job?"

"Looking for something." He tensed. "No, no bird. It's just complicated."

"If it isn't a woman, what is it? I can't help if you don't tell me."

"Who asked you?" the man questioned belligerently and lapsed into unfriendly silence.

Watching the man and the rifle with careful but still nonchalance, Order realised with surprise he was not afraid. This fellow wouldn't hurt him, not deliberately, because whatever was worrying him it was not John Order or anything he stood for. He was not a political crank, someone with a grudge agin' the government, politicians in general or authority itself. He was too removed from such passions.

The real risk was an accidental discharge of the weapon.

"Sorry, didn't catch that?" Order became aware the man was speaking again.

"D'you know something called Moby?"

"Can't say I do. Know where it is?"

"Just asking."

"Look, I don't know why I'm here or what you want," Order said in the following silence. "What's your problem?" He risked leaning forward confidentially.

"Forget it!" The man rose quickly, almost upsetting the ashtray at his feet and dislodging a piece of paper on the arm rest.

He was out of the room heading further into the house by the time Order cautiously settled back in the chair.

John Order, newly elected Member of Parliament, was thinking about a rush to the front door when he heard an unmistakable crack that if it wasn't a firecracker was a shot.

＊ ＊ ＊

Two hours later Order was thinking of making the same rush, except that he had no chance of success this second time. The police were everywhere.

"No sir, I'm still here."

The plainclothes officer turned away so Order could not follow the conversation on the mobile telephone. The interruption gave him time to reflect again on what he had seen.

The man's body had been sprawled against the cheap fibro of the bathroom wall, between the toilet and a stained old bath. With the rifle barrel resting against his left thigh and both legs half bent in the same direction, he looked like a sleeping soldier from one of the paintings in the Australian War Memorial further across town.

The bloodied head dispelled this gentle impression.

Order had never seen a dead person before, yet he was detached from any special feeling. He didn't know the man and although it was a shabby way to die beside a grubby bath that was the situation and he knew what he had to do.

As Order had explained to the policeman, he had not checked the man's pulse because there was no sign of life from the body but had gone promptly to his car to telephone the authorities. Fortunately, because he had almost finished the block, the vehicle had been around the corner.

"Why didn't you have the mobile with you?" the young policeman had asked, bewildered why anyone would separate themselves from one of life's necessities.

"I don't like carrying it on door knocks. It's something else to cart around an' any call I do get could have waited."

He didn't mention the mobile was a bulky old-fashioned unit given to him as a new member by penny-pinching bureaucrats. It sat uncomfortably in any pocket in which it was placed.

"Why not use the 'phone in the house?"

A trace of suspicion perhaps in the policeman's question?

"I didn't think about it an' my own was nearby. An' I didn't see one."

"In the kitchen," said the officer.

He had driven back to the house after making the call, experiencing an odd thrill at the secret he still held against all the neighbours as he pulled up in the silent drowsy Sunday afternoon street.

Inside again he checked the body and noted that the time was three thirty five, which didn't mean anything because he couldn't remember when he had been first bailed up.

Now waiting for the police he was reluctant to sit down again, although he knew he would not disturb any evidence by doing so. It was standing self-consciously in the middle of the tatty lounge-room still uncomfortable from the cigarette smell that he noticed the paper beside the dead man's chair.

It was not his business card, which Scots forebears frugality would have urged him to retrieve, but parts of a printed logo like you see on company letterheads.

Moby Investments, he read, then a section of a post office box number.

On impulse Order pocketed the paper and he felt its edge now as the policeman told him his boss was coming to continue the interview.

Detective Inspector Williams must have been on his way when he 'phoned through because he arrived within minutes. He was a big man with patient eyes and the Canberra nous to know that dealing with a politician, even a possible oncer, called for tact.

"You say you were door knocking the neighbourhood?" he began and Order once more explained his 176 vote majority.

"You say you heard a shot?" continued Williams, when Order again explained how he had come to be in the house. "What did you do then?"

"I explained that too to the other officer."

"Nobody else in the house?"

"Not as far as I was aware."

"No noises for example, which might indicate the presence of someone else?"

"No."

"And after the shot you investigated and found the deceased in the bathroom?"

"You didn't look around the rest of the house?" Williams continued upon his reply.

"Why should I? There's a body in the 'loo an' I'm the only person in the place."

"Let's go through it again, if you don't mind, Mr. Order." Williams' tone was deferential but still skeptical.

"Well I don't need to detain you any longer," Williams said after Order had repeated his story and the dead man's failure to elaborate upon the 'complications' which had brought him to the National Capital.

"No upcoming interstate or overseas committee trips, Mr. Order? It's just that we may need to get in touch again."

"No, but I'd like to be kept informed."

"Of course."

Williams did not sound very convincing, thought Order as he walked into the street where the setting sun was casting long shadows.

The body must still be inside, he decided, because an ambulance was parked in front of his car and a group of neighbours were clustered on the other side of the blue and white police tape. A television crew was the other obvious indication all was not yet wrapped up here.

"Mr. Order?"

The young woman was smiling from a pretty face above a severe high necked green suit. The Canberra television stations had oddly formal dress codes for weekend reporters, he thought, silently composing himself for the interviews to come, because the woman now was joined by other newshounds.

"How do you feel, Mr. Order?" the interviewer began and he briefly considered saying full face into the camera: "Like shit. I've just seen a dead body. How can you ask such a dumb question?"

But he didn't.

Rather he remembered the advice of Bernie, the Party secretary, that held more members talked themselves out of parliament than into the place and so kept his remarks short and guarded. Simply why he had been there and what had happened and yes, how shocked he was at such a tragic death.

He said nothing about the slip of paper in his pocket nor the dead man's interest in something called Moby, reasoning these were not matters which should concern the insatiable public.

Nevertheless, he wondered why he had kept the same information from the police.

TWO

At the regular Monday morning Party meeting Order noted reactions were mixed about his weekend adventure. In the casual talk preceding Fearless Leader's arrival and the beginning of business there were a few joking references to law and order - a new but also resurrected play upon the parliamentary uses of his name which had tiresomely dogged his first few weeks in the legislature.

By and large those most generous were the members with safe seats while a touch of envy permeated the comments of those in the marginal constituencies, envious of the free publicity he had garnered even in the national media. Order again was reminded of Bernie's truism that in politics you had many acquaintances but few friends.

Being a non-sitting week the meeting lasted longer than usual, with backbenchers raising issues they had not had the chance to bring up in the tenser and time precious gatherings before the insistent bells summoned them to the Chamber.

The level of crime was a perennial subject for the right wingers.

"It comes to a pretty pass when one of our own is held up in broad daylight while simply going about his lawful political duties," topically complained Paul Severin, a capital punishment advocate.

"Hope it doesn't encourage copycat behavior," Order's friend Rob Glasson interjected, taking some of the heat out of the criticism.

"I wasn't in any danger," Order protested.

"You can't be sure an' anyway there's no way we will ever find out. Was he black, by the way?"

In the ensuing hubbub of protests from Party moderates Order wondered if the police had called with more information and at the end of the meeting hurried back to his office.

Elizabeth or Liz, his middle-aged secretary-cum-electorate assistant covered the mouthpiece of the telephone.

"More media," she explained. "This is the fourth this morning. Almost worth a media conference?"

"Tell them we'll get back. I'll need to clear it."

Shadow Ministers - as they liked to style themselves - often had announcements they wanted or needed to make and did not take kindly to backbenchers stealing their publicity opportunities. After a couple of big party room arguments following such political gazumping, it was decided public statements by non-executive members needed to be cleared by the media relations section or MRS: universally known as Mother Hubbard.

Like many apparently sensible procedures the instruction was viewed with suspicion by most backbenchers, who saw it as a ploy to deny them constituency exposure. The mavericks, who liked to display their independence of the Opposition executive, also saw it as censorship because the MRS always wanted a copy in advance of the statement to be issued or the comments to be made.

Leaving Liz to her telephone caller Order went through to his cluttered private office, its walls lined with rapidly filling book-shelves, the desk trays brimming with paper.

No matter how thoroughly the efficient Liz sorted the twice daily mail delivery, removing the A to Z of magazines, journals and newsletters which gratuitously found their way to him as a parlia-mentarian, there still remained a sizeable collection of correspon-dence definitely requiring his attention. Inevitably, there also was an equally large though smaller quantity which could be important and therefore needed his careful personal reading.

Liz, divorced with grown-up children, which was a common circumstance in affluent Canberra, liked to mother Order, or so he believed, but she wisely never tried to think for him.

There were four yellow post-it stickers on his desk pad.

Bernie, the Party secretary, Jim Terry the media officer he shared with several other backbenchers, someone called Betty Downer and yes, Inspector Williams.

"Said you wanted to be kept informed. Deceased was an A-l-a-n Todd," the policeman began in the stilted way they're taught to speak. "We're continuing our enquiries in Sydney but I don't see it as anything more than a straight forward suicide. You'll be needed for the inquest probably." he continued and hung up.

Bernie was as brief and succinct.

"Play this for all it's worth, John. Not many Opposition back-benchers get the chance for this type of favourable publicity."

"But I haven't done anything."

"That's what's great about it. No awkward questions. Just a good local member getting on with the job of meeting his constituents."

"I've got to ring Jim Terry."

"He's probably had the same idea. Tell him to push the visual stuff; television and a photo of you for the print media. And then…" Bernie paused.

"An' then? Sixty Minutes or maybe CNN?"

Bernie's laugh was mirthless.

"Nothing so flash, John. Quite the opposite in fact. Back to door knocking as quickly as you can, while they still remember your face and your little adventure and before the football heroes take over again."

Bernie was nothing if not focused.

A balding cardigan-wearing chain-smoker - in defiance of occupational health and safety rules - Bernie was shy in person but very effective on a telephone.

He had been of great help to John Order following his pre-selection and through the long and chaotic election campaign, advising, directing, organising and yes, occasionally boosting sagging morale. So much so Order decided Bernie had taken a shine to him, the novice political aspirant.

It was Rob Glasson, now serving his second term, who put him straight.

"Bernie's the same with all of us, John. A total political animal. You're as special as all of our candidates with a chance of winning an' when you do, you're just as special to Bernie to keep you there. Even if you stuff up he'll fight in your corner, 'though don't be too sure you'll get another bout if he thinks you've damaged the Party."

Order telephoned Jim Terry and they agreed that the media's insistent follow-up requests were worth seeking a clearance from Mother Hubbard for a media conference or at least a public statement.

Terry was another of Bernie's ideas. All backbenchers had a staffing allowance they could use as they saw fit. Like most members, Order allocated the bulk of this money to pay Liz, with a smaller portion to a part-time office assistant, a university student, who worked a set number of hours per week maintaining constituent files, updating the list of addressees for the planned quarterly electorate newsletter and doing whatever odd jobs needed doing.

Since his 176 vote defeat of the Government's nominee, Order also had the enthusiastic support of a small group of local volunteers who would fill envelopes for pamphlet drops, accompany him at Saturday morning shopping centre Meet the Member visits and, more occasionally because they preferred anonymity, sign letters to the newspapers extolling his worth as the electorate's political representative.

This still found Order short of a media adviser.

The Opposition executive was reluctant to seek additional funding for extra staff. Although the decision for more money was made at arms length - as every politician was quick to point out - by the fiercely independent Remuneration Tribunal, that body only responded to written submissions from parliamentarians and these pleas could become available to an ever critical media.

So no deal, no more money for staff. Not if you wanted to win the next election.

This expedient decision saw Order as a newly elected and in-experienced member at a disadvantage in the labyrinth of media relations. Fortunately, he was not alone.

Bernie, his political nose scenting victory for the Opposition next time around, realised there were a number of backbenchers with no political savvy for dealing with the fourth estate. Indeed, most could not even prepare a tight, lucid and eye grabbing media release.

Bernie examined the staffing allowance and found most back-benchers had annual money unspent. Not enough to employ someone, but by pooling these amounts …

Hence Jim Terry.

Order looked at the last post-it.

"Liz. Who is this Downer woman?" he called. "There's no 'phone number. What does she want?"

"One of your door knocks on Sunday, she said. Called in from a public telephone. You said you'd look at her back fence? Anyway, she wants you to."

"You're right, I do remember, 'though not the fence." Order also remembered the clipboard was still in his car, forgotten in the drama of the warm weekend afternoon.

Still, and in spite of Bernie's insistence he resume door knocking as soon as possible, it was Tuesday afternoon before he pulled up in front of the Downer's monocrete guvvie, similar to most in the street save for the different approaches to the garden, which ranged from carefully tended to jungle to barren parking lot.

The Downer's fell somewhere between neat and neglected, as if increasing water charges and age had defeated them. Because he re-membered her now, a short plump older woman behind a fly screen door, initially suspicious about his visit - as most people were - then a little incredulous to see a live politician on the doorstep and finally mild confusion about how to take advantage of the opportunity presented.

"John Order," he announced. "You called yesterday. I'm sorry I couldn't contact you about this visit."

"Oh Mr. Order, thank you for coming. It's perfectly alright you calling like this. Since Cyril died I haven't had the need for a telephone an' I don't go out much anyway. Come in, please."

A small entrance hall, lounge room to the left, the wall to the right screening off one of the three bedrooms, laundry and back door probably dead ahead with kitchen left and bathroom right. In spite of Bernie's cautions, he'd seen a number of standard government owned houses.

"Would you like a cup of tea? I don't have coffee, I'm afraid."

"No thanks, Mrs. Downer," Order was pleased he'd established her widowed status in this age of feminist minefields. "I've come to look at the fence?"

"Of course. Come through."

And Mrs. Downer led him straight ahead into the laundry and through it to the back door.

"There," she said, as if revealing something special.

The grass needed mowing, except for a small area around a sagging Hills Hoist and the overgrowth climbing the chassis of a car.

"My son's," Mrs. Downer said, catching Order looking at the vehicle. "He lives in Adelaide now but I see the grandchildren when they all come over for Christmas."

The fence, thought Order, blocking out the wistfulness in her tone, something as a bachelor he could not and did not want to appreciate.

Very grey, very old, with concrete uprights cracked here and there to reveal rusting iron from water seeping in and expanding over numerous hot summers. One section of the fence was sagging, where a cross beam had come away and enough palings were missing for a person to climb through.

"I've spoken to the department two or three times, Mr. Order, an' nothing's been done."

It was the government's responsibility to replace fences of Housing Trust properties. If the fence shared a common boundary with another Trust house, the government paid the total cost of replacement, if the boundary was shared with a private residence, then the cost too was shared.

This was the rub, because you could not always obtain agreement from a private owner that replacement was necessary.

"And who owns the house behind you, Mrs. Downer?"

"It's Betty an' it's Housing Trust too, Mr. Order." she said, patiently he thought, and then added: "But I thought you knew that already, seeing as that's where you saw that unfortunate man shoot himself."

I didn't see the back of the place, Mrs. Downer, Order thought defensively, squinting uphill to a very untidy backyard.

"Anyway, I do hope you can get my fence repaired, Mr. Order," Betty Downer said proprietarily. "I'm sick of people up there using my yard as a quick way to the shops."

Seeing his puzzled expression, the woman explained that while there was a laneway linking her street to the local shops one block below, there was no corresponding laneway linking the street above.

"This house is directly opposite the lane to the shops, Mr. Order, an' because they don't have any gates up there an' since Cyril died an' I sold the car I don't have any gates either an' because there's holes in the fence, people treat it like Pitt Street."

"Used to be just kids, y'know," she continued, warming to her grievance. "Now everyone does it."

"Surely it can't be that regular?"

"Well, it's pretty regular, Mr. Order. I had one same afternoon as you were here. Saw you on TV about it. Bold as brass he was. Came down through the yard, through my fence, carrying a golf bag, though why you'd want to walk to Yowani from here, I don't know. Get enough walking on the golf course itself, I'd think."

Order tried to keep his voice casual. "And what time would that have been, Mrs. Downer?"

"Oh, about three, I think. Yes, about three, because I went into the kitchen to make tea after the fifth race at Flemington an' I saw him through the window. Bold as brass he was."

THREE

Order knew where he was heading; nevertheless he drove slowly going over the full conversation with Betty Downer.

Yes, the man had been hurrying but not as fast as to draw attention to himself. No, she couldn't describe him in detail. Certainly tall and thin, wide brimmed hat and sunglasses and casually dressed like you would be for a game of golf, including gloves – golf mitts, Order decided. And no, she couldn't swear he was or was not a regular who used the shortcut to the shops.

"But you see why it's so important to have the fence fixed, Mr. Order."

As he pulled up outside the death house, Order saw his suspicions had not been misplaced when he'd seen washing on the line beyond Betty Downer's troublesome fence. Washing that was not the late Alan Todd's unless the man had been a cross dresser.

An old and battered yellow Toyota sedan was parked in the gateless driveway.

The woman who answered the door was unhealthily fat, her weight straining against a pink top and black track suit pants. Order tried to forestall the question by presenting his card.

"I thought you were the cops again," she began, confirming his ploy had not worked. "But they're usually in twos. Wait, you're the bloke with Alan, I saw you on TV last night."

"That's me, Mrs. ..."

"Boone - with an e."

"Mrs. Boone. I was wondering if you would answer a few questions."

"About Alan? I've told the cops all I know an' identified the body or what's left of it. I took the kids to the coast for a few days to see their father, my ex. Came home Sunday night to find the place under guard."

They were standing in the lounge room, now so familiar to Order. It was less tidy and Mrs. Boone searched around for cigarettes and a lighter before replying to his next question. Although he didn't like cigarette smoke he felt he couldn't object in her own home.

"Alan Todd was an old friend an' I put him up for a while. I don't know why he was in Canberra."

"How long had he been staying?"

"Couple of days. Why?"

Order remembered Todd had said he'd been in Canberra a couple of weeks. He could have moved around but it was more likely Mrs. Boone was sub-letting and did not want the Housing Trust to find out. Theoretically a breach of tenancy but impossible to police. Order didn't think it had anything to do with Todd's death.

"Any visitors?"

"No. Went out a bit but didn't say where."

"Get any mail?"

"Hardly." Cautious now. "Only here for a few days, not as if he'd moved in."

"You said he was an old friend. You knew him in Sydney then?"

"Yeah. Years ago. Went out a couple of times, I think."

"Did he mention anybody called Moby? Maybe a company of that name?"

"Yeah, he did, but I couldn't help." She drew on her cigarette. "Why are you asking all these questions anyway? You're not a cop."

"I spent some time with him, Mrs. Boone. In this very room. I just wanted to get to know more about him. It seems a sad way to go. Alone like that."

"Yeah. Well he's made things difficult here. The kids don't want to use the bathroom anymore. Difficult enough getting them to use it before this happened, now it's almost impossible. I have to go with them."

"He didn't leave anything? Papers perhaps?"

Mrs. Boone was on another tack, her eyes became distant.

"Cops took everything, though there wasn't much. But look, if the kids are frightened of the bathroom d'you think this could get me a bigger house? I've been asking Housing for months because I've got four an' its only three bedrooms. Three boys an' Sherri-Ann growing up, it's not decent them sharing."

Order wondered where Todd had laid his head but his thoughts were interrupted.

"An' you're my local politician, aren't you? Can you help me with Housing, Mr. Order?"

"I can certainly try, Mrs. Boone." And because he needed to escape the thickening cigarette smoke and saw the chance to check out a growing suspicion. "Perhaps we could even extend this property? Is there much room at the rear of the house?"

A hallway ran back from the lounge room, bedrooms both sides, then the bathroom and laundry to the left, kitchen to the right. It was an ugly design but, just as he thought, the back door stood at the end of the hallway.

If someone had hidden in the nearby kitchen and if that someone was the short-cut golfer, then possibly Order was looking at a murder and somewhere a murderer.

"Just one more question, Mrs. Boone. Did you know Alan Todd had a rifle?"

"Do you think I'd have let him stay here if I did?"

FOUR

As he drove along the still silent street, another note to his clipboard, Order decided upon a more direct approach.

A quick call to Liz established no telephone book listing for Moby or Moby Investments so he took himself back to his parking place and walked across Civic to the Office of the Registrar of Companies. Cheaper fees had attracted many businesses to register in the A.C.T. in past years and although the saving was not as great now, the national capital retained most of its interstate clients, including Moby Investments.

Clearly it was inoperative, a shelf or two dollar company with the address of a firm of large local solicitors Order thought recently had amalgamated with yet another equally large law company. Moby Investments listed three directors: Richard John Melville and Wilga Irene Melville, both of a ritzy area of Canberra, and Terrence William Hagan of Darlinghurst, New South Wales, which Order knew to be an inner Sydney suburb.

Neither of the Melville's was known to him, something which might have caused no comment in a larger city whereas in a Canberra of only half a million residents it still was possible for people in certain business, professional or social brackets to be well acquainted.

He noted the residential address anyway, promising to drive by when next in the area. Perhaps he would know somebody who was a close neighbour.

For the moment however, parliamentary duties required him to spend the remainder of the afternoon and early evening in committee, listening to the wearying predictability of successive community groups trying to make a case for more government funding.

With his colleague Wendy Wonder - or Wendy the Wonder Woman as she was known privately in defiance of one or another of the discrimination laws - winning the brownie points for the Opposition over the efforts of the three Government members to mollify the witnesses, Order thought about what he had learned and what he should do next.

He was totally inexperienced in this field. The sensible thing was to hand it all over to Inspector Williams. Let the police sort it out.

But what did he have to give them? Betty Downer's information about a golfer taking a shortcut at a convenient time? Todd's reference to Moby something? A piece of paper he should have given to the authorities that could link Moby with Todd?

And which he had not done.

It was now clear to Order he had two choices: either hand over everything he knew - and presumably some of which the police did not - and risk public criticism or worse, ridicule, for his dilatoriness. Wanted the publicity, didn't he, rang in his mind. Or he could privately stay with it, at least until matters became clearer or they didn't. In which case he could drop the whole business with no harm done to anyone, especially himself and his political future.

"Mr. Order is in full agreement, I'm sure."

Wendy Wonder's strident voice interrupted his thoughts.

"Of course," he confirmed.

"That concludes the meeting," the chairman, old Jim Rhodes said with an emphasis Order realised meant he had missed something again.

"Mr. Chairperson, I think we should extend this hearing for another thirty minutes," Wendy the Wonder Woman suggested, playing to the witnesses across the table.

"In fact, I so move."

"Ms Wonder, the hearing is fixed to conclude at six-thirty. Other members have commitments even if you don't," Rhodes said angrily.

"I moved the extension, Mr. Chairperson. I insist you put it to a vote."

"Very well! Those in favour of an extension of thirty minutes? Those against? Motion lost! This hearing stands adjourned until next…"

Rhodes was annoyed Wendy Wonder had forced a vote upon an adjournment and Order realised even if the government always made sure it had the numbers on any committee, it was still possible to procedurally outmaneuver a majority even if most politicians regarded the tactic as petty and time wasting.

Any appreciation of Wendy's performance did not survive the return to his office.

"You just missed him, John," Liz said, using the familiarity they practiced in private. "An' he didn't leave a message."

"Who didn't leave what about what?"

"A man rang as you rose from the hearing," which Liz obviously had been monitoring on the internal television network. "Said he wanted to talk to you about Alan Todd's death."

"An' didn't leave a message."

"That's what I said."

"Okay. Try to hold him if he rings back an' give him my home number."

Order's election inconveniently had not coincided with the pre-publication entries for the yearly telephone directory listings and he spent a lot of time and effort distributing home and office numbers. Being publicly anonymous was not a circumstance relished by a newly installed parliamentarian.

"You've got your select committee at seven-thirty," Liz reminded him.

Committee work was a chore given to new backbenchers. Rarely did their membership provide them with the publicity that was a politician's lifeblood, unless they cut up really nasty at a hearing. This behaviour risked alienating witnesses, particularly if they were bureaucrats, who might then hold a grudge through into government or even ministerial preferment.

So most junior committee members served out their apprenticeship politely and in relative silence until the ebb and flow of political fortune gave them a chance for stardom.

The committees, known as standing or permanent, originally had been set up to mirror ministerial portfolios and usually consisted of five members; three government and two opposition. The election of independents and smaller party representatives altered this simple balance but the government always made sure it had a majority.

Occasionally the government allowed a select committee to be established to look at a specific issue. These committees were especially unpopular because they cut into the established routines of meeting days and times of the standing committees and often their references were well outside the expertise or even interest of their membership. Whips were rumoured to use them as punishment posts for members who had offended in some way.

And select committees usually sat at inconvenient hours simply because no other time was available.

This led Order reluctantly to the parliamentary dining room, now a sad parody of former glitter and glory.

Old hands reckoned it was the increasing number of women in the parliament; others blamed a more health conscious society or the drink driving laws. Whatever, the dining room looked more like a dry canteen these days and the cartoonists' depiction of bloated pollies' stuffing themselves with food and wine was tired, hackneyed, wrong and still widely believed.

Although mineral water predominated, alcohol was not entirely unknown and Rob Glasson was sharing a glass of red with Tim

Forbes, the opposition's police spokesman, when Order joined them.

"So how's the hero?" Forbes asked.

"A bit puzzled an' glad to see you, Tim."

"Why?"

"The suicide. A constituent might have thrown doubt on that theory an' I don't know if I should report it."

"To the police? Who's handling it?"

"Fellow called Williams."

"Gabby Williams? Big bloke, sleepy eyes?"

"Well yes, I suppose so, but I wouldn't call him overly talkative."

"That's why he's nicknamed Gabby, John, because he doesn't. Probably the most laconic man I know."

"So what did you find out?" Rob Glasson asked, signaling for his account.

Order explained between mouthfuls of lasagna the shortcut golfer's appearance about the time of Todd's death.

"Reliable constituent?" asked Forbes.

"Seemed so. Elderly, widowed, but Betty Downer's observant for her age."

His two companions glanced at each other, broad and pitying grins giving way to controlled chuckles.

"Didn't waste much time, did she," Tim said to Glasson.

"She phone you up, John?" asked Rob.

"I door knocked her."

"Walked right into it. Oh well, you'd have to meet her eventually."

It was a matter of amusement to the more seasoned politicians when tyros like Order made initial contact with one of Canberra's characters.

"We've all dealt with Betty, John," Rob Glasson explained. "She's a regular complainer an' she loves latching onto the new chums, probably because the rest of us won't help her anymore. What is it, footpath or does the house need painting?"

"Back fence repairs."

"That figures," interposed Tim Forbes.

"She's genuine. The fence needs repair."

"Of course. Look Betty's okay. She's not crazy like some of them. She just always wants something for nothing."

"But what about this golfer?"

"Just adds a bit of colour to her request," said Rob, pushing back his chair. "Don't let it worry you. Drop a line to the department through the Minister an' let them decide about the fence."

"Good advice, John. I'm off too, see you tomorrow."

Suddenly Order's lasagna was cold and stiff.

FIVE

It was almost eleven o'clock when a weary Order let himself into his flat.

While outside the electorate - a political minus Bernie nagged him about - the address was close to the parliament. One bedroom, a bathroom, lounge-living room and a rarely used kitchen provided him with a compact, reasonably comfortable domicile much cheaper than the ambitious three bedroom residence on the quarter acre block of his brief marital fling.

Politics could be devastating to personal relationships, just ask anyone outside of the parliament trying to date someone working inside it, but Order thought in his case religion and children probably had as much to do with the marriage breakdown as long parliamentary nights and unfounded suspicions about the temptations of staff bimbos. At least he could be thankful the matrimonial foray had ended while he still was a staffer and thus avoided any possible fallout as a member.

As he glanced beseechingly at the telephone, its red message light unblinkingly returning his gaze, Order thought again how bloody and frustratingly careful a parliamentarian had to be. Forever assessing, weighing up the risks, deciding what to say and when to say it. He knew his temper and the need to control it but no wonder most voters believed their elected representatives were two-faced liars.

He hefted his briefcase onto the occasional table beside his favourite chair, only then realising he still was holding the mail he had collected outside a few minutes earlier.

And again as he flicked through the garish brochures and envelopes he reminded himself to buy a No Junk Mail sticker for the letterbox. He was so busy throwing the unsolicited paper into an untidy heap at his feet that he almost missed it.

A small cheap envelope of a type sold in supermarkets across the country, it had been delivered by hand because there was no postage stamp and more interestingly, no address. As he tore at the flap, Order wondered uneasily how many people in the darkness outside could accurately find his letterbox in this flat complex.

Stay out of this, he read on the single sheet of white paper.

Order was knocking upon Mrs. Boone's door shortly after eight the next morning.

"You pick a fine time to call, Mr. Order. I'm getting the kids off to school." She turned back into the house. "Derek, you'll be late!"

"Just one question. Did you tell anyone about my visit earlier this week?"

"Only the other cop. Came just after you left."

"And asked what I wanted? Among other questions, of course."

"Well yeah. Something wrong?"

With only a rudimentary description which would fit most middle-aged, non-balding suits in Canberra, Order reassured an increasingly distracted Mrs. Boone everything was okay and no, he hadn't forgotten her request for a bigger government house.

Back in the office he rifled unsuccessfully through the telephone messages.

"No, sorry. Education." he explained in a brief call from Rob Glasson, declining his invitation to lunch and was looking through his appointments diary for an alternative date when the function caught his eye.

"Are you going to the Business Development drinks tonight?"

It was not a question you asked most of your parliamentary

colleagues and those you did ask, you didn't ask often. Childish really, because everyone would be invited, yet the same everyone all secretly hoped the next invitation would be exclusive to them alone. Not asking occasionally saved embarrassment too when someone hadn't been invited.

Order asked because he knew Rob, as a business liaison task force member for the Party, was certain to be on the guest list and Order was hoping to meet more of the local business community's movers and shakers. In this he was conforming to Bernie's aphorism that in politics you only have acquaintances not friends, so use them.

Education was the usual dogfight with the committee split upon political lines over the recurring topic of corporal punishment. Order nevertheless had to work hard to keep Julie Davenport, his Opposition colleague, with him upon the need to allow individual schools an option whether or not to permit it. Julie was a do-gooder who thought everything in education at the grass roots from spitting in the playground to slitting someone's throat at recess could be resolved by counselling. He sometimes wondered what she was doing in the Party at all - and he was not alone.

After the rigours of the committee meeting and a stop at his office to draft replies to constituents - Order was not into dictation and neither was Liz - he was more than ready for the Business Development drinks.

Nevertheless, he willed himself to be patient, idling away the time marvelling at the assortment of even Liz censored afternoon mail across his desk: expensive interstate seminars claiming to improve his management skills, invitations to local functions to consider a challenging cross-section of social issues, glossy magazines from trade associations throughout the country and notices of community meetings in the electorate. All of these groupings usually made up the bulk of the correspondence. Occasionally there was a constituent letter, however these contacts now were increasingly by facsimile or e-mail.

There were no more warning-off letters.

The Business Development drinks venue was within walking distance of the legislature and he allowed himself ten minutes after the appointed time for his arrival. Order was new to representative politics but he liked to think he learned quickly. Hence don't be too keen to arrive. It looks as if you have nothing better to do or you're a drunk.

The room was moderately full of suits of both sexes and Order forced himself to slow his walk so he could pick out someone he knew to join, all the while fighting a rising panic that tried erroneously to convince him he knew nobody present.

Both government and opposition politicians were scattered among the crowd but he knew better than to join any of them. As a last resort perhaps, but even a first term member was expected to make their way unaided socially after the first couple of months in the job.

He was deciding his options while surveying the drinks range of red or white wine, beer, orange juice or mineral water, when a deep voice boomed behind him. Harold Chambers, the elderly white-haired Opposition Whip, beckoned him to join a small group.

"You know all these people, John?"

Rumour had it Wendy the Wonder Woman was after Chambers' job, but if so he was a sly old devil Order decided, noticing Wendy herself standing with the Whip.

"Barry -"the surname was lost in a burst of laughter nearby and Order accepted the proffered business card.

"I don't think we've met," said a second man, also presenting his card. "I've heard of your recent exploits though. I'm Dick Melville."

"Leave you to it, John," said Chambers, nodding Wendy in the direction of another group and for once Order did not resent being used as a substitute.

The man was of average height, clean shaven and dark hair. He looked like the late aged thirties businessman he probably was.

"And what do you do, Mr. Melville?" The card Order held simply identified Moby Investments and Galaxy Investments.

"Dick, please. Development, construction, commerce and retail properties. Pretty varied really."

Barry Whoever had wandered off and Melville suddenly leaned forward, saying in a low voice that he'd like to catch up with Order soon.

"Certainly. How about 'phoning my office. My secretary can check the diary."

"I'll do that. Now, if you'll excuse me ..."

Order looked around the increasingly crowded room where there were plenty of people he could join but he could not see Harold Chambers anywhere.

He'd wanted to ask the Whip if Melville had contrived the introduction to him, then realised it didn't matter. Order himself probably had let on more than he thought he had when he failed to ask Moby Dick why he wanted to talk with him.

It was then the speeches started, destroying the pleasant ambience of the evening and, at their merciful conclusion, Order joined the drift to the door.

SIX

No matter how early he arrived at the office - and Order was an early riser - Liz was there before him, opening the mail and checking the day's diary of appointments and meetings.

This morning was no different, however he noticed the chamber pot had been moved.

Actually it was a large bowl inherited along with the office. Nobody knew what it was for and while disrespectfully christened the chamber pot, it served a useful purpose because if moved from its centre position upon the occasional table inside the door it alerted Order someone unexpected was waiting to see him.

Because the position of the bowl could be seen from outside, Order simply kept walking and entered the suite by the private door further along the corridor. Known as the escape hatch, this entrance and exit opened into the member's private office. It didn't matter if the unexpected visitor saw you slipping past; you at least had time to prepare for the meeting or confrontation, as the case may be.

Escape hatch offices were popular with ministers and members alike.

Order was reaching for the telephone when he saw the post-it note.

Police 0805, it read.

"Show them in, Liz." he called through, guiltily grateful they had only been waiting ten minutes.

"DI Williams, Sergeant Shanks, Mr. Order," said the big man, preceding Liz. "We met over Alan Todd's death."

Order nodded, recognising Shanks as the officer he had first spoken with at the death house and motioned them to sit down at the conference table, a low circular item of government issue beech furniture matched by surrounding chairs of surprising comfort and height.

"Coffee?"

"No thanks, Mr. Order. I hope you don't mind us turning up unannounced, but you did ask to be kept informed."

"Of course."

"Not that I've much to tell. Rifle registered in Todd's name an' fingerprints are being checked now. D'you want the technical details?"

"I know nothing about guns, although I'd like to know where it came from."

"Had it with him."

"Mrs. Boone swears he didn't. She wouldn't have let him stay if he had."

"We'll look into that," Williams nodded to Shanks who wrote something in a pocket size notebook. "Anyway, post mortem showed nothing suspicious, 'though you might have been lucky."

"Lucky? Why?"

"Because Todd was moderately intoxicated. Whisky."

"I didn't see a glass -"

"Probably interrupted him out in the kitchen or somewhere. An' you're lucky because the rifle didn't go off."

"Did you find a glass?"

"Don't rightly know. There was nothing in the lounge room, as you said. Did you find one, Sergeant?"

"No sir." Shanks obviously took after his boss in conversational brevity.

Order explained the sighting of the golfer leaving the property about the time of the death.

"So you think Todd could have been drinking with this person when you interrupted them, Mr. Order?"

"Why not? An' as you suggest, the drinking session could have been in another room of the house. If it had been the kitchen, would you people have paid much attention to a couple of glasses in the sink? It *looked* like a suicide."

"What about the bottle?"

"Was there a bottle, Inspector? What if our golfing friend took it with him in the bag?"

"Hold on, Mr. Order," Detective Inspector Williams finally decided to defend the professionalism of his officers. "Just because someone takes a short cut through a property about the time someone else dies there doesn't make for a crime."

"Coincidental 'though, don't you think?"

"So what? Anyway, we've only the word of your witness as to the time. Is he reliable, would you say?"

"She. Yes, I'd say Betty Downer is reliable. She's a widow and like many old people living alone she doesn't miss much."

"No. Betty Downer, if she's the one in Milperra Street, certainly doesn't miss much," Williams said depreciatingly.

The Australian Capital Territory, in which sat the planned city of Canberra, enjoyed a unique advantage over other cities around Australia and, as far as Order knew, the world.

This advantage was a boon to visitors and a particular convenience to knowledgeable locals: no two avenues, crescents, circles, circuits, closes, drives, lanes, places, roads, rows or streets had the same name. People who lived in Canberra and knew an area thus could identify its residents and whereabouts confident they would not be misunderstood nor would they mislead.

"You mean Betty Downer's known to the police?"

"No, no Mr. Order," Williams explained. "Known *to* the police is the wrong expression. Betty Downer is known *by* the police."

"She's a nuisance," he added.

"A common assessment."

"And a correct one. Betty Downer is known from probationary constable up to the Commissioner. She contacts us about twice a month to complain about something. I assume from what you've said her current gripe - if you haven't fixed it - is people using her backyard as a short cut to the shops. Right?"

Order nodded.

"Then just fix the fence, Mr. Order. Please?"

Williams stood up.

"We've taken enough of your time and yes, I'll have our records checked for a bottle and glasses somewhere." Shanks made a note. "Meantime, as I came to tell you, we'll probably only need a statement from you for the inquest. You're a busy man."

As indeed he was.

"You decided to drive out to the Finnegan's about the parking problems," Liz reminded him as she replaced the chamber pot.

"Not the Finnegan's, their street," Order corrected mildly. After the ear bashing he had received upon the making of the complaint Order had resolved to conduct any future business with those angry chatterboxes exclusively by mail.

It was good to be out of the office. If Order had been asked what he most liked about his job it was this type of constituency work that he would nominate every time.

Driving across Commonwealth Avenue Bridge, unidentifiable flags announcing a State visit or some special national or territorial activity hanging limply from their poles in the warm sun, the vista of Federal Parliament House rising before him, even the talkative Finnegan's seemed an acceptable cross to bear.

It was not the political big picture that interested him and nor did he believe it interested the majority of the population. They just wanted to get on with their lives with minimum fuss, inconvenience and interference. Big picture activities usually meant big money which ultimately was provided by them, the taxpayers.

No, parking, litter, bad roads and ugly graffiti usually were the concerns of the electorate and Order was very prepared to address such grassroots issues.

Turning off to the left toward the imposing National Library of Australia, Order realised these mundane matters upon which the electors sought action also included fences in need of repair.

His confidence in Betty Downer had taken a hammering and from people whose knowledge and experience he believed he must respect. Yet if she was only a lonely old whinier, how could he dismiss the threat in his mailbox?

Of course the anonymous warning might have nothing to do with Alan Todd's death. There were plenty of cranks around who were easily offended, although he couldn't recall any recent contentious issue involving him that might have provoked someone.

And this was because like most backbenchers and despite the efforts of Jim Terry, it was difficult to gain approval of Mother Hubbard for more than a very occasional media release. The shadow ministry distrusted backbenchers, who they saw as being ignorant of the grand strategy and much preferred them to stick to quiet day-to-day constituency work, leaving the public statements to them, their more knowledgeable betters. This way too the backbenchers did not become a threat to their positions.

His publicity from Todd's death had been his first media appearance for weeks, which made Order think that there was some connection with the back-off note and the dead man, irrespective of Betty Downer's respected detractors.

It was with relief Order swung into the Finnegan's street and began the slow careful drive between the cars parked against both curbs in selfish defiance of safety and suburban amenity. Anything to save parking fees, he thought contentedly, knowing he had a grassroots problem to address.

SEVEN

Another heap of junk mail behind him in the wastepaper bin and John Order found the party room meeting offered much of the same.

It was surprising how gossip occupied most of the members' time while waiting for the meeting to begin.

Today the Leader of the Opposition was late and Order learned Wendy Wonder had been re-nicknamed Volkswagen.

"Saves time," explained Rob Glasson. "Wendy the Wonder Woman is just too long. Abbreviate it an' you get WWW or three W's or VW, hence Volkswagen, get it?"

"Haven't you anything more important to think about?" Order asked.

"Yeah. Is she screwing our Whip?"

"Oh yes, very cunning," added Tim Forbes, slipping into the seat beside Glasson. "She's ambitious but I don't think she'd go that far."

"She'd have to provide the Viagra. He's a skinflint."

Further salacious discussion was interrupted by the arrival of Fearless Leader and the official business of the meeting commenced.

Order's junior status among even the backbenchers gave him a silent listening role. That at least was Bernie's advice: don't try and set the world on fire too early in the party room son, you'll only burn your fingers.

Already however, he had begun to experience a small and growing confidence as he saw the way the members' played their roles.

Some were very circumspect, careful to present balanced arguments to issues, others of both moderate and conservative persuasions, were very direct. It seemed to depend upon whether or not you wished to win a decision on a matter coming before the parliament or simply to make a point - a warning even - to your colleagues.

Parliamentary parties he knew are fragile coalitions of individuals with strongly held views. Opinions often are voiced within the party room as a caution that to go too far in a particular direction will invite trouble. An intelligent leader recognises these signs and will seek to reach a consensus, realising there is a constant ebb and flow of loyalties, support on this issue, opposition upon another matter.

Unity in the House, even silent or sullen unity, is all that ultimately counts but one must be appreciative of the undercurrents elsewhere.

"I cannot see why we should take a soft line," Paul Severin argued. "The wretched boy was defacing the building for the third time. It was his tag. That's why he had his arm broken."

"And his face pushed into the wall, then sprayed with the rest of the pressure pack," complained Julie Davenport.

"The chattering classes go spare about this sort of thing," continued Severin, "and no doubt there'll be a hand wringing editorial sometime soon, but the truth is that ordinary decent citizens want firm action and discipline. This is the third time the Galaxy's walls have been defaced and in the absence of any real support from the Courts; the manager took the law into his own hands."

Amid mutterings of vigilante justice, weak law enforcement and the need for more education of juvenile offenders, the party decided to examine tougher penalties for graffiti offences and moved on to the next item of business, while Order wondered if there was a connection.

Within fifteen minutes of the meeting acrimoniously breaking up, Liz had the answer.

"Three restaurants, John. Woden, Tuggeranong and Gungahlin. Surely you've seen the not very original TV ads: Galaxy, for out-of-this-world food?"

Order, who like most politicians watched very little television except the nightly news when he could, had a vague recollection of space type pictures.

"Anyway," Liz continued, "you can ask the man himself. Dick Melville's invited you to a barbeque next Sunday."

"So he did follow up."

"And you can go, according to the diary. Give the door knocking a miss. You'll meet just as many people at the Melville's, I'd reckon."

Sitting at his desk signing off letters to ministers or sending their replies on to constituents, Order wondered what the invitation really meant. Apart from a torn scrap of paper, there was nothing to link the Melville's with the death or suicide of Alan Todd.

The barbeque simply could be the Melville's catching up with a newly elected politician, a public relations exercise very widely employed by many of Canberra's more successful and canny business leaders.

He was flattered. That someone should have sought him out after a mere three months in the parliament was promising and that that person, Dick Melville, was obviously a local businessman of importance was even better. Maybe his political career was moving forward at last.

Order had experienced a degree of disappointment ever since the heady euphoria of his 176 vote by-election win. It was, he knew, his own fault because while his victory had been claimed as evidence of the party's resurgence, it was a 24 hour media story and then the political heavies who joined him so enthusiastically during his campaign had returned to their real strategies for defeating the government.

Like having children, politics called for no special skills, no licence, no real character check and no financial sustainability.

You were sworn in if successful, allocated an office, provided with a motor vehicle and given a staff allowance. If you were lucky someone like Bernie was around to give you advice and someone like Rob Glasson was there to show you the political ropes. You also had a tour of the parliamentary precincts and a briefing session by its officials.

Nevertheless, Order remembered the confusion of the first few weeks and the lonely days and nights as he largely found his own way through the thickets of parliamentary life.

As a former staffer this was a surprise, because like bridesmaid to bride there were significant differences, of which in his new station lower status was but one.

An opposition backbencher, even a by-election giant killer, quickly learned that as a tyro member his tactical advice so much sought after as a backroom minder was no longer of importance. He was now in the front line, not behind it.

He found he was not privy to information as readily available to him as a staffer. Confidences too were not exchanged and other members were loath to help a new chum with campaign tips for fear of giving away something unique which might in future be too widely broadcast and as a result become commonplace.

Constituency letters, for example.

Signed by local residents extolling the candidate were now so much a part of normal campaign tactics as to be worthless as a newish election tool.

Politics demands the loyalty of all except those who practice it for a living, Bernie had once observed.

Fortunately, apart from volunteering homespun advice, Bernie also was of practical help. It was he who found Liz and so created order for its namesake in his office.

Liz was super efficient, had worked in parliament before she'd married and possessed a sensible approach to office management. Soon the filing system and daily diary were up and operating, a means of tracking constituent requests was established and various ministerial offices began to recognise the blue coloured memo which indicated a reply to correspondence was overdue.

Starving opposition members on action for their representations was not unknown, but with Liz it declined dramatically. In a break with the usual approach to dealing with electoral requests, Liz sent a copy of Order's letter to the minister on their behalf to the constituent, who could then decide for themselves who was holding up a reply.

Thinking of Dick Melville's Sunday invitation jogged a memory. Order picked up the telephone.

"What's happening to Todd's body?" he asked.

"Good question," replied DI Williams. "Normally next-of-kin but I'm not sure there is anyone we know of."

"Could you find out, Inspector? I'd like to attend the funeral." Order lied.

Williams was back to him faster than Order expected.

"There's a wife in Sydney," he said apologetically. "My sergeant had all the details and seeing it's a straightforward death, he didn't bother me."

"So he's going back there?" Order asked, ignoring the inference.

"No, he's being cremated here. Those are the current instructions I understand, when we release the body."

"Would you keep me informed an' when I'm to appear at the inquest?"

"I don't think that will be necessary now. As I said, it's straightforward an' the less media hungry publicity - by which I mean your presence Mr. Order - the better."

"Call me John," Order said impulsively.

"Gabby," conceded Williams, hanging up.

EIGHT

The Melville's lived in an expensive house in old Canberra, where the trees were so established their overhanging branches gently touched across the cool streets congratulating each other's survival from developers.

The building itself was a rambling single storey which, unlike the nouveaus in the newer suburbs, did not have to garishly proclaim the owner's success. There were several cars in the circular drive and many more parked outside in the street.

The deliberate ten minutes late, he wore the Canberra weekend rig: slacks, loafers, open neck shirt and coat, the latter preferably with brass buttons. It was a uniform much favoured by important people seen on weekend television and said unequivocally I've been interrupted on my day off but okay, I'll sacrifice a few precious seconds giving your audience the eye benefit of an interview.

Order paused momentarily where a path forked off the pebble drive toward the rear of the house. He decided to follow it because that was where the noise came from and he didn't fancy hammering upon the open front door to attract attention.

Rounding the corner of the building he was confronted by the backs of about 40 people. Of the actual barbeque there was nothing to be seen.

"Mr. Order, so pleased you could make it," Dick Melville came toward him from a group just as he tentatively moved forward.

As was a prerogative of the host at casual weekend gatherings

Melville wore no coat, otherwise he was dressed identically to his guest.

"Let's get a drink an' I'll introduce you around." Melville gently propelled Order to a makeshift bar in front of closed double doors leading off the slate patio, where they picked up glasses of white wine from an obliging waiter.

"Come on, I'll introduce you," Melville repeated, leading him into the crowd.

Order noted the female fashions ranged from sensible to very casual and that the women were mostly young to middle-aged.

All except for a very large matronly blonde who looked to be much older and waited watchfully with a younger man as Melville and Order approached.

"My mother, Wilga, and my brother Terry," announced Dick. "This is John Order, who won the by-election a few months ago."

"And was more recently a hostage, I recall."

The woman, Wilga, was as tall as Order, which made her statuesque. The hair was not the blonde he had thought but white from her sixty plus years, which also had added weight to her body and an extra chin to her face. These obvious signs of age were not evident in her bright intelligent eyes.

"It must have been terrifying," she continued, when Order agreed.

"I'm sure Mr. Order doesn't wish to be reminded of the incident, mother," interposed the man at her side.

Terry was of similar build and colouring to Dick save for a growing and thickening black moustache, which gave him a 1940's movie star glamour. Also, he was more casually dressed, wearing slacks and a T-shirt with what appeared to be a crossed rifles logo on the left breast.

"I think Mr. Order can speak for himself, Terry," Wilga Melville said sharply and stood waiting for the reply.

"I didn't really feel afraid, Mrs. Melville. I just didn't think Alan

Todd would harm me. I can't explain, but he didn't seem to me to be dangerous."

"Except to himself, Mr. Order."

"Perhaps."

"Perhaps? He shot himself, Mr. Order." The intelligent eyes coolly engaged his own. Dick and Terry listened silently.

"Yes, well that's what the police think."

"And what do you think, Mr. Order?"

"Well, I can't argue with the police, I suppose. They're the experts in these matters, aren't they?"

"I have no idea, Mr. Order, but I should *imagine* they have the necessary experience to make a correct judgment. Wouldn't you agree?"

"Yes, I suppose so."

Wilga gave a tiny smirk, as if a small but troublesome matter had been resolved to her satisfaction.

"I mustn't keep you talking any longer, Mr. Order, I'm sure there are lots of constituents here you would like to meet. Richard, if you and Mr. Order would rejoin us for the lunch."

As they moved back toward the other groups of guests, Dick expressed an opinion Order had already reached.

"Formidable woman, my mother."

"And your brother, Terry?"

"Not quite right, Mr. Order. Half-brother actually, but as you've noticed we're very alike. The moustache helps people tell us apart, although there's not much call to do so now."

"Howso?"

"Terry lives in Sydney, so we only get mistaken for each other when he's here on a visit. D'you know Tom and Rebecca?"

Order was flattered to find he was the only politician present and enjoyed, however briefly, being shepherded around by Dick until summoned to Wilga's table for the meal.

"We call it a barbeque, Mr. Order, but it's really just an outdoor hot buffet," Dick explained, as they lined up to have their plates laden with steak and sausages, grilled tomato and browned onion rings by another hired attendant. "The salad is this way."

Terry must have served for his mother and they were both garnishing their food when Order and Dick Melville arrived at the round outdoor table.

"Here Mr. Order, sit beside me." It was not a request but a command. "Richard, pour our guest some wine."

Sitting beside Wilga, Order had an uninterrupted view across the lawn and the tables where other guests were gathered. What struck him as unusual was the dress of most of the people.

Unlike the smaller group to whom he had been introduced before lunch, the men wore gaudy beach shirts, shorts and thongs or denim shirts and jeans. While their wives and girlfriends - plump, relatively ordinary looking for the most part - sipped at wine, the men nursed stubbies of beer and, once the food was collected, used their knives like spears to cut it up.

If the eclectic mix puzzled Order, he didn't dwell upon its significance. A politician and especially a new member welcomes any chance to move and meet outside the comfort zone of committed supporters. The initiative would have to wait however, because Wilga engaged him again with questions about the hostage drama.

"How long were you held in that house, John? You don't mind me calling you John, I hope?"

"I don't rightly know -"

"Wilga, please."

"Wilga. Todd didn't like me moving, not even to look at my watch."

"How dreadful. But what about conversation? Did you talk together or just sit like two statues?"

"I tried to get him talking but he wasn't very communicative."

"He must have said something," said Dick from his right.

"Just that he was looking for something an' it was complicated."

"What was complicated?" Wilga again.

"I don't know."

"How very mysterious," wondered Wilga.

"Maybe or maybe he was just a crazy person," said Terry from Wilga's left. "Either way we'll not find out now. Seconds, anyone?"

Order glanced at his watch and saw he had been here almost an hour and a half. In the unofficial rules of political function attendance it was time to leave. Not good being among the last, again it showed you either had nothing else to do with your time or you were just another drunk.

"Thanks. I really must be going. I'm door knocking this afternoon." he lied.

"Oh, what a pity," Wilga said unconvincingly, then brightened. "But we must have a photo first. Terry ask Gonzo to take it."

So Order posed with Wilga and her sons while the thick-set bullnecked Gonzo, who looked like he'd be more at home behind a mechanical shovel than a camera, took a souvenir snap.

"I'm sorry I didn't have a chance to circulate," apologised Order, then realising how self-interested that sounded he clumsily added: "I should have given you more time too Wilga, to mix with your guests."

"Please don't worry, John. These are all our employees. They don't need nor want me getting in the way of some serious drinking. Didn't Richard tell you this was our annual staff barbeque?"

"I don't recall so."

"No matter. They're all very loyal to me so being here won't do your political career any harm. Richard, see John to his car."

"She's like that sometimes, a real lady of the manor," Dick said as they threaded their way through untidy tables where empty beer stubbies were accumulating.

"Your mother an' Terry are part of your business?" Order asked a question which had been puzzling him.

"It's a family company."

"Just you three directors then?"

"Yes."

If the responses did not then the tone in which they were delivered left no doubt Dick was not keen to discuss the subject.

As he maneuvered his way through the cars and utes parked on both sides of the street, Order wondered why he had not asked his second question, the one about the late Alan Todd's possession of a piece of the Moby letterhead and the link, if any, with the Melville's.

NINE

With the House in session this week, Order had no time to think about the implications of the barbeque in the suicide or murder of Alan Todd.

A sitting week changed the atmosphere of the parliament. There was a tension in the air, urgency in matters requiring action and a perceptible shortening in tempers, at least among the major players.

The party room meetings became exclusively focused upon the business of the sitting day, first Tuesday, then Wednesday, finally Thursday with a very occasional special Friday. Speakers lists for the scheduled debates were drawn up and those who needed to know were told to be prepared if the strategy committee determined the unexpected was called for, such as a Matter of Public Importance. Those lucky enough with a turn to ask a question were either provided with the question if tactics demanded a concerted attack upon one minister or had their own question vetted for its political benefit by the committee. Nothing was left to chance.

Order found this concentration upon the political jugular disturbing. Not being directly involved, he could not understand the blood lust of the party's star parliamentary performers, while as a newcomer to the House he was still a populist, much more interested in the issues affecting his constituents and the opportunity to air these matters in Question Time.

He was rostered for a question this week and was dismayed when his own choice was brushed aside by the strategy committee and replaced with a finance question of such obtuseness Order knew he would have to practice the delivery just to sound convincing. He hoped there was some real point to asking it and not a case of one of the backroom boffins showing off.

The longer, strained party meeting and the loss of a precious constituency question time slot put Order well out of sorts and the mood was not improved when he returned to his office.

"An inspector called," Liz said wittily. "Nobody remembers a whisky bottle at Todd's place, although there were several dirty glasses in the kitchen sink. He also said the cremation is at Norwood Park tomorrow at two o'clock."

"So I'll need a pair," said Order, wondering if he'd get lucky and also miss asking the unintelligible question.

"If you want to go."

"I would and I will. The government's usually generous about giving leave for funerals and I think I owe it to him, Liz."

Thus Order found himself sitting at the back of the sunlit room watching the coffin slowly disappear from sight on another warm Canberra afternoon.

Apart from two suits across the aisle, who could have been police despite Williams' contention the death was straightforward, and Mrs. Boone several rows ahead, Alan Todd was going to his eternal rest unmourned save for the crematorium staff.

And the woman in the front row left.

In the embarrassed hush as the music faded, the suits quickly departed followed by Mrs. Boone after she glanced briefly at him and spoke quickly to the woman. Order stayed, intrigued by the stranger's presence.

As she came toward him he saw a woman of late thirties and of medium height. Her face framed in blonde short-cut hair was beginning to show the onset of middle age or perhaps it was strain, nevertheless she was attractive in a disheveled careworn way.

"Thank you for coming, Mr. Order," she said in a husky voice as she reached him, "I appreciate your kindness."

Seeing his bewilderment, she added: "I'm Alan's wife, well widow I suppose. Monica."

Order's bewilderment was replaced by shock now Monica Todd was standing before him. She had the most beautiful eyes, a blue which sparkled. In spite of the hushed surrounds and the reason for being here, Order found himself captivated by their liveliness.

He was mumbling a condolence when she asked if they could talk somewhere privately.

"I appreciate you coming to the funeral, Mr. Order," she began, stirring her coffee as they sat under the trees of an empty post-lunch café in Lyneham, "and I have a favour to ask."

"I don't know anyone in Canberra," she explained, "Alan and I met after he moved to Sydney to hit out on his own -"

"Which was?"

"About three years ago. Anyway, I've never met the family here and I don't really know how to start."

"Why?"

"I said how quite deliberately, Mr. Order," Monica Todd said, raising her dancing eyes to his own, "because it's complicated."

"That's what Alan said," Order blurted out. The black clad figure was full and topped by the blonde hair, Monica Todd was attractive in a definitely sexy way. Order was grateful he was a bachelor, because if something eventuated here his public position would not be threatened.

"He came here to try to sort matters out," she continued. "To make them see reason."

"Who?"

"His family, the Melville's."

"You mean Wilga, Richard and Terry? Those Melville's?"

"The same." Monica brushed tiredly at her short hair.

"It is complicated and I understand your confusion, Mr. Order.

Alan's name is Todd because he was the only child of a short-lived marriage - at least I think they were married - before Wilga met and married Melville."

"Melville treated all the boys alike but genes dictate, I suppose. Alan was different, he was not a businessman, had different interests and when Melville died he decided to pursue them, so he headed for Sydney."

"What were his interests?"

"He wanted to paint, Mr. Order."

No wonder he went to Sydney, Order thought. The local cultural scene outside the Australian National University was notable for a lot of wine, crowded openings, short-lived exhibitions and prodigious efforts to obtain government subsidies. The artistic community inspired little confidence, limited talent and much unintelligible jargon and bitchiness.

And you were his model, decided Order.

"That's how I met him. I did some modelling. I was slimmer then," she concluded, looking down at her body self-depreciatingly.

"This career path didn't please the Melville's?"

"No way. He became the family's black sheep and they didn't want to know him."

"Was he a good painter?"

"I'm no judge but he didn't sell much. At first that didn't seem to matter, he was so excited and happy about breaking away from the family and doing his own thing. This bohemian independence made him a very attractive person - to me anyway - but as time went by and critical success eluded him, well he became the way you saw him, I suppose."

"He looked tired," Order said kindly.

"Yes, I can imagine. And with long hair? Drinking perhaps or smoking something? The longer he was unsuccessful, the more Alan reverted to the character of the penniless artist. Although we weren't in a garret, finances were tight until I found a decent job."

"And that hurt Alan's pride," she continued. "So he decided to come to Canberra to get his payout from the family."

Monica explained under the terms of Melville's will the estate was divided into four parts, a quarter share each for Wilga, Richard, Terry and Alan.

"Mr. Melville placed no restriction on the quarter shares being taken out; in fact the will was silent on the point. This encouraged Alan to come to Canberra to obtain the family's okay for him to take his twenty five percent."

"Was he successful?"

"I've no idea. Whether he saw them or not I don't know. He wouldn't stay with them. He said his self-respect wouldn't let him, but I think he was frightened his stepmother would talk him out of taking his share. That's how you ran into him."

"Why would Wilga talk him out of taking his share? From what little I know there's plenty of money to go around with the Melville's."

"Except there could be more," Monica folded her arms under her breasts and leaned forward across the table. "Old Melville did make one stipulation in his will and that was if one of the shareholders died their share didn't pass to the next of kin but to the remaining shareholders. I think he meant well, Mr. Order. It was probably intended to keep the estate with the three boys should Wilga remarry and then die before her husband. However, the result has left me broke."

The result also is a motive for murder, thought Order.

TEN

He drove slowly back to the House, the mild excitement of his meeting with Monica Todd making him a careful motorist.

As a politician Order was cautious about involvement with women, although as a bachelor he had less to be concerned about than his married colleagues.

Nevertheless, there were pitfalls.

If you were seen with one woman only, gossip soon made you an item and expectations rose about you making legal whatever was going on, if you had several women among your friends then you were a playboy, while to act safe and be seen alone you were gay. Unquestionably it was more convenient to be married, provided the union was stable and your spouse accepted the rigours of political life.

Even in his short time as a politician Order was surprised to learn how many spouses were less than supportive of their partners and was left wondering why the budding politicians put themselves forward in the first place.

Lack of marital support created its own dangers within the parliament buildings, work stations to pretty and impressionable young secretaries, research assistants and media advisors, while the electorate itself had its share of enthusiastic political groupies.

Order knew the key to getting involved in any affair, even for a bachelor, was discretion.

Which was why he was attracted to the possibilities with

Monica, a convenient not-too-demanding involvement with an out-of-towner was the stuff of most men's fantasies. This also was why he had promised to stay in touch.

It was bad luck the House was sitting; otherwise he could have asked a lonely Sydney visitor to dinner.

The thought came as he locked the car and made to maneuver himself sideways against Eddie Brown's badly parked Commodore. If Monica by her own admission was broke, who paid for her visit to Canberra and who paid for the cremation?

The parliament's pairs were time generous and he was not required for duty until after the dinner break so he went directly to his office.

"Mrs. Downer's 'phoned about getting her fence fixed," Liz said placing the afternoon mail upon his desk. "I told her we'd get back to her."

Pity it had been a door knock, Order thought, quickly sorting most of the correspondence into the wastepaper bin. If Betty Downer had telephoned the original request he could have asked her to put it in writing. According to Bernie you never again hear from nine out of ten callers if you ask them nicely to write a letter. The sincerity test he called it.

His fingers stopped shuffling through the papers at a cream envelope marked personal.

The thick heavy feel of it turned out to be two pieces of cardboard sandwiching a photograph of Order with Wilga, Richard and Terry at the barbeque.

On the back a strong hand had written ambiguously: *Hope you enjoyed this function too, Wilga.*

The warm fantasy feeling Order had carried away from his meeting with Monica was gone. Looking at the words and the smiling foursome John Order realised he was compromised, because the photograph was designed to lock him in as a mate of the Melville's to anybody who happened to view it and read the comment.

His anger at this contrived predicament was mollified when the Opposition Whip's office telephoned with the news the evening sitting of the House had been cancelled.

It happened from time to time, usually as a result of more protracted delicate legislative negotiations than the parties involved had anticipated. Few members saw the free night as a bonus however, because they knew it would have to be made up sometime in the future. With the House sitting pattern decided for convenience sake twelve months in advance, adding an extra night meant cancelling some other activity generally in the electorate. The Whips hated the extra sittings because everyone wanted a pair to fulfil these previously made commitments.

For once Order wasn't displeased with the change and wasted no time contacting Monica Todd.

"I'm sorry it's such short notice," he apologised, detecting the slight hesitation even after he had explained what had happened.

"No please, it's very kind of you," the husky voice assured him. "It's only that I'm expecting a call about seven - from Sydney," she added, as though an explanation was needed for an attractive young widow receiving a telephone call in a city where she knew nobody.

"So you've no idea if your late husband met his family when he came to Canberra?" Order asked later.

Monica Todd had not changed her clothes but she looked less tired and the candlelight of the restaurant table increased the sparkle of her eyes.

"No. In fact I don't recall him speaking to me about them at all."

"How long was he here?"

"Two or three days, I think."

Monica Todd noticed Order's eyes narrow.

"Mr. Order," she looked down at her glass then raised her beautiful eyes to his own "perhaps I should explain that Alan and I weren't living together when he came to Canberra. We hadn't been for a while and I've no idea how long he was here in town. I've no reason to lie about this, I simply don't know."

"There was no special reason for our separation, you understand. Alan had just become difficult to live with as his career increasingly went nowhere. We stayed in touch, of course, and then one day he 'phoned to say he was coming down here for his share of the money."

"But according to the will you say the share reverts to the other three. How can you claim anything, Mrs. Todd?"

"I suppose I'm hoping for an ex-gratia payment - and please call me Monica, seeing as I'm telling you confidences."

"Why should the Melville's do that, Monica?" Order asked, relishing the newfound intimacy.

"Because I was Alan's wife and I think they would like to get rid of me out of their lives."

"For someone who hasn't met any of them you seem very sure of a strong position."

"I am John," she smiled away the liberty, her eyes flecked with light. "Although I haven't met them, Alan told me enough. Wilga's the real boss in the family, always was even when old Melville was alive, and she's very strong on status. The last person she'd want challenging her social position here is an ex-artist's model like me."

A great thing about Canberra was the second chance it gave so many people. In the boom days of an earlier forty odd years it was possible to come to the then overgrown country town and make your fortune through hard work in construction and then property. While it was tougher now, the competition was nowhere as fierce as in Sydney or Melbourne and in Canberra having made it most people wanted to flaunt it.

"So you think they'll buy you off?"

"I know they will." Again she leaned forward, her hands crossed under her undeniably attractive and promoted breasts, "but I'll need help."

"Howso?" asked Order, trying to concentrate upon her face.

"I don't know them, John. I need an intermediary who has met them. Ideally someone important and who they regard as important, to plead my case. Someone like you."

He'd seen it coming, Order agreed to himself, as the waitress fussed around setting down the main courses. Right from the crematorium meeting.

But it made sense too. How could this attractive widow now waiting earnestly for his response, successfully approach people like the Melville's without help? And it wasn't much to ask, he was simply effecting the introduction. The bargaining was Monica's.

"I'll think about it," Order said like any cautious politician, guiltily wondering what personal advantage he could ring out of this woman for the service.

"Thank you, John," she leaned across and gently squeezed his hand with her own, which he noticed wore no wedding ring. "I thought I could rely on you."

"It might take some time, Monica. How long are you staying?"

"Home tomorrow. I thought I should bury Alan here, at least near his family, even if they didn't come to the funeral. But I'm a working girl and I have to get back to Sydney."

"I'll need a contact," Order began.

"Of course," Monica reached to the slim black handbag at her elbow, extracted a pen and business card and wrote something detailed upon the reverse.

"There," she announced, "even my home address."

Was there a promise in the remark, he wondered, noting a unit or flat in Bondi printed upon the back of the card of an insurance company in Sydney's CBD.

"And the funeral, Monica. Who pays?"

"Oh they will, John. I'm sending the account to Wilga."

Suddenly her face softened and her voice took a lower husky tone.

"That must have sounded callous. In fact I've probably come out of this whole conversation sounding like a greedy vengeful woman. I'm not really, it's only that I think Alan deserves more than a quick unattended cremation and a three way split of his estate and so do I as his widow."

Her eyes no longer sparkled but locked onto his own in mute appeal.

"I can't blame you wanting financial justice considering the way Alan died."

Now Monica's eyes narrowed.

"The suicide?"

"If that's what it was," Order said quietly and sat back as the waitress removed the remains of the course and produced the menus for dessert.

"What do you mean?" Monica whispered after they had ordered two coffees.

Order believed in being honest, a trait Bernie complimented him upon by postulating that while being honest could get you into trouble, being dishonest ultimately got you into a whole lot more: "People might not like your honesty, John, but hopefully they'll respect you for it."

At the end of his story, including Mrs. Downer's sighting of a stranger in the backyard about the time of the shooting, Order added lamely: "I hope this possibility won't prejudice your chances."

"Of money?" Monica passed her hand across her forehead. "No, I don't think so. The Melville estate isn't insurance, so murder any more than suicide wouldn't stop the settlement. But who would want to do such a thing?"

"Someone getting a greater share of the Melville money, perhaps?"

"I see what you mean, but it seems a bit drastic. There's plenty for everyone, I understand." Monica looked at him quickly, as if remembering something. "Have you told the police?"

"Yes, but they're sceptical. I can't blame them, there's no hard evidence except the word of a known nuisance."

"That I can understand."

"I hope I haven't upset you with this talk of possible foul play. I didn't want you to hear of it and my obvious involvement by accident, if it did turn out to be true."

"No. And I thank you, John," Monica gave him a small smile. "It's better I know this now. The prospect of Alan being murdered shocks me, of course, but it sits easier with me too." She paused. "Is it because it's a more honourable way to die, something largely beyond your control?"

When Order didn't reply, Monica traced a pattern on the tablecloth with a finger nail, thinking, before she continued: "I'd be fooling myself and lying to you if I didn't admit Alan was at the end of his tether. If he couldn't get his share of old Melville's money, I think he'd have done himself in anyway."

Monica, don't torture yourself over this, Order thought, and asked to get away from her possible loving feelings for the late husband: "How about more coffee?"

"No thanks, John. I've an early start back to Sydney. I'd like to go back to the motel if you will."

In the car she returned to the subject as they drove through the largely empty main thoroughfares of Canberra midweek.

"You must think me calculating and unfeeling, John, to have such a detached attitude to my late husband, but if you'd known him when I met him, so full of fun and confidence and then the way he just gradually fell apart."

"Don't talk about it, Monica."

"I owe it to myself, John; otherwise you'll think me a cold bitch. I'm sure our separation didn't improve matters but even before then his moods, his drinking and smoking God knows what, made him much less than he was." Monica turned to Order. "And I think he knew it too, John, and didn't want to live at that level."

He concentrated on turning into the motel car park.

"That's why I can't feel or at least express the grief I think is expected of me, because I know his death, whatever the means, was inevitable if he couldn't get his money."

"I'm not judging you, Monica," Order pulled on the handbrake and turned to the widow, her face dark in the overhang of the upstairs footway.

"I know, but it's important to me that you in particular understand, John." Monica leaned across and kissed him softly upon the lips. "No, don't get out; I'm right in front," pointing with her key. "Thank you for dinner and everything. I hope I can see you again soon?"

Order watched as she opened the door to the motel room, trying to make sense of her comments and her actions and deciding they hopefully added up to promise.

ELEVEN

With the parliament not sitting until ten thirty and thus the party meeting an hour before, Order's early arrival at the office gave him ample time to consider his next moves with and on behalf of Monica.

Although he'd only done so once, he knew it was not difficult to get out of town and with Sydney three hours easy drive upon taxpayers provided petrol; there was not much cost involved.

The situation changed when the House was sitting and his chest tightened at the realisation he could not hope to go to see Monica before the following week.

And he did want to visit her, to further and develop their contact at a more personal level than the telephone. The pretext would be to report on a visit to the Melville's acting as an intermediary as Monica had requested.

He made a note to Liz to set up an appointment and was rifling through the overnight e-mails when he saw the barbeque photograph in the Too Hard tray.

With half an hour to the party meeting Order thought he could manage it and was soon driving steadily against what passes in Canberra for morning peak hour traffic.

At Mrs. Downer's he wasted no time showing the elderly woman the photograph.

"You take a good picture, Mr. Order."

"Thank you, but is there anyone else you recognise?"

"I don't think so. The man with the moustache looks familiar, but I don't know anyone with a moustache these days," said Mrs. Downer doubtfully, peering closer.

Driving back to the legislature in thicker traffic Order congratulated himself his hunch had paid off. While not wishing to put ideas into her head, he was convinced under his gentle prodding Betty Downer had almost recognised Richard or a clean-shaven Terry, despite wide-brimmed hat and sunglasses, as the golfer using her yard as a shortcut the day Alan Todd died.

Pity it wouldn't stand up in Court.

Being the second last sitting day for two weeks, the party meeting was all business. The government was keen to have several items of legislation passed before the fortnight's adjournment and the opposition equally keen to intelligently oppose or sensibly amend the proposed laws, so conversation and debate was focused again upon the daily Notice Paper.

With the unpredictability which is so much a part of politics, Order found himself with a busy day: Chamber duty in the morning, his question reinstated for Question Time and third speaker, if required, on an education amendment.

It was not until the lunch suspension he returned to his office where Liz told him Wilga Melville would see him Monday afternoon. So with luck he could drive up to see Monica later in the week.

"Don't forget tonight's residents' monthly meeting," Liz reminded him and Order now recalled her words as the chairperson - for it was that sort of meeting - droned on. Was it because they liked the sound of their own voice, he wondered, that some people insisted upon reading aloud their own previously circulated report or did they think everyone else present was illiterate?

Among the thirty or so members of the public, Order also identified three of his parliamentary colleagues. They too had the vacant switched-off look of a person enduring something boring, but he knew this to be deceptive.

Each of the politicians in attendance was watching the others, watching and listening and he knew if one spoke, they all would speak, because it was the unwritten rule. No matter they had been acknowledged already by name so the audience knew they were present and thus carrying out their constituency duty, none of them was about to allow any other politician to however briefly publicly occupy centre stage.

"Any questions arising from my report?" the chair asked hesitantly.

And of course there was, because again in Order's albeit short experience public meetings usually attracted a person who knew as much as or more than the holder of the position. Order expected the questioning, although he would have pumped for it to follow the treasurer's contribution - there was always a financial expert - and was patiently waiting for the man to finish, while thinking more of Monica than the issues of this boring gathering.

"... and so the Galaxy restaurant will not occupy the site?"

"I understand negotiations are continuing with the government," the chair attempted to reassure him.

"That's not much of an answer. Some of our representatives are present, maybe they can bring us up to date?"

Canberra had no third tier of government, usually referred to as council or municipal, so the legislature handled all the local planning proposals as well as State-type responsibilities.

Order cursed silently. There was no way all elected representatives here tonight could avoid being dragged into the discussion. One in, all in faced with the few but noisy ferals of an apathetic community.

Order himself had little to contribute and wisely followed Bernie's advice: he said what he had to say and sat down.

What did interest him however, was Edward 'Teddy" Beare's defence of the government's handling of the issue.

Galaxy restaurants *were* owned by Galaxy Investments and

therefore from Beare's robust support far from being opposition supporters, the Melville's obviously had a foot firmly planted in both political camps.

TWELVE

This betrayal still lingered as he swung the car into the Melville driveway the following Monday afternoon, breaking quickly to avoid rear ending the unusual sight of a *dirty* 4WD parked in suburbia.

At least it indicated someone was home, he told himself, pressing the doorbell a third time and wondering, as he did often when door knocking, if the mechanism was broken or disconnected.

Order's relief when the door was opened was mixed with surprise. The thickset bullnecked Gonzo, the unlikely photographer, glared silently at him.

"An appointment with Mrs. Melville," he explained, accepting the wider opening of the door by this brooding man as an invitation to enter.

Gonzo silently led him deeper into the house to a large sitting room off the main hall and indicated, by pointing a stubby finger; he should sit down in one of the uncomfortable looking armchairs facing a rather explicit painting of *Leda and the Swan*. Gonzo moved to and opened a door opposite the hallway entrance.

"Thank you Gonzo," he heard Wilga Melville's voice say dismissively. "Would you come through, John?"

Order found himself in a boudoir, complete with double bed and vanity table, where Wilga sat doing something to her face. She was wearing a white terry towel robe, high heeled shoes and, he suspected, little else.

Most male politicians had at least one story of a scantily clad woman, either fresh from shower or bed, and a few even unchivalrously embellished their experience with an apocryphal ending. Political groupies do exist but this was the first time John Order had encountered one of the rare sought after species.

"Now what can I do for you, John?" Wilga turned as she spoke, a broad smile almost as inviting as her deep cleavage.

She was not unattractive, if a little on the heavy side, nevertheless his political alarm system was ringing in his brain louder than the division bells at the parliament. He looked around for somewhere safe to sit before beginning his plea for Monica.

"Do excuse me, John," Wilga rose and swept across to the wide bed. "I was about to take a nap. I'd forgotten our appointment. Please forgive me. You sit on the vanity chair and I'll prop myself on these pillows."

And so she did, showing an enticing amount of a well-proportioned long leg.

Order could hardly believe his situation, which was anything but conducive to the appeal he had come to deliver on Monica's behalf.

Trying to ignore the generous flesh, he explained the purpose of his visit and Wilga heard him through in silence.

"That woman is trouble, John," she announced, adding at his obvious confusion: "Yes, I know her and I've received the account for Alan's cremation, so your visit was not unexpected."

"So what do I tell her?"

"I won't see her, John. There's nothing to discuss. Under the terms of my late husband's will the estate reverts to a three way split in the event of a death among the original foursome. Surely Monica would have told you this?"

Order could do no more than shake his head.

"What she didn't tell you I'll wager, is that she wanted Alan's share of the estate for herself to set up a hairdressing business I'd guess, because that's her background. But she could only access it while Alan was alive. Monica sent Alan to Canberra to claim his share of the family company, however he dies. Now she can only make a widow's plea, using you John, to test the water. Well, it's cold."

Wilga paused. "You're not married, John?"

"Not now."

"Neither are my boys."

She swung herself off the bed, rescuing the fallen half of her robe and covering the exposed leg.

"Let me show you something."

She bent across the vanity, ignoring the amount of ample breast she was revealing. It was as if she had given up on trying to seduce him and now was occupied with something far more important to Wilga Melville.

"Our original happy family."

The photograph had been taken outdoors and some years previously because an older man, presumably the late Mr. Melville, stared defiantly at the camera from atop what looked like a fence rail. Grouped around him were Wilga and the three boys.

And Monica.

"She said she'd never met the family."

Wilga's chuckle was throaty.

"I said Monica was trouble, John."

She stood the audience at an end.

"Gonzo will see you out, John, and tell him I want him afterwards, please."

"Mrs. Melville wants you," Order said truthfully and Gonzo produced a brief smile.

THIRTEEN

"**W**hy didn't you tell me?"

Order had thought a lot about how he would confront Monica and the evasion, not to say outright lie, she had delivered. In the boring two and a half hour drive on the freeway to Sydney, he constructed several approaches and toyed with plans, ambushes really to catch her out. The strategies also were designed to control his temper.

He himself hadn't been forthcoming when he telephoned to say parliamentary business was bringing him to town. He justified this behaviour because he needed to see her reaction to his information. He also thought he had a fair chance of bedding her this time.

The opportunity didn't look so promising now in the somewhat cramped lounge room of a 1950's Bondi Junction flat.

"I don't know," Monica admitted. "I thought it might be easier for you to speak to Wilga without knowing I knew them."

"It put me at a great disadvantage," he said with heat.

"I see that now and I'm sorry, John." Again, as in Canberra, the eyes fluttered an appeal.

"Well, it didn't change anything. Wilga won't see you," Order said with relish but his anger softened when he privately admitted his reaction was really the embarrassment of not knowing her relationship with the Melville's.

"Not surprising after the way I behaved to Dick."

"Alan you mean."

"No, Dick," Monica's eyes widened, seeing his puzzlement. "Oh God. She didn't tell you then?"

"Wilga only said you were trouble, Monica," Order said challengingly.

He waited while the barefoot jeans and T-shirted woman turned away seeking perhaps inspiration from the wall. Abruptly Monica walked from the room and before he could recover from this new surprise he heard the unmistakable sound of a refrigerator door opening and closing. Then she was back, two stubbies in her hands.

"We might as well sit down," she said, handing him a beer with no offer of a glass.

"The reason I wouldn't go to Wilga myself," Monica began, holding the unopened bottle as if she had forgotten about it, "was because of Richard, or Dick if you prefer, who I knew was in Canberra."

"I was married to him once," she added quietly.

Order took a long pull upon his beer, grateful for the excuse not to comment.

"The cause of the break-up was a lot of things. We were too young, Richard too tied up in the family business - these reasons are unremarkable, I suppose - but then there was Wilga herself. The old matriarch. She didn't see me as her daughter-in-law, she saw me as an addition to Melville Enterprises, specifically as the producer of the next generation and heirs. She was stifling and Richard, knowing which side his bread was buttered, did everything she asked. Well almost, anyway."

"Almost?"

'Except give her grandchildren. God knows we tried hard enough, but no go.'

"Did you seek medical advice or help?" Order found himself using his constituent interviewing tone.

"No. Richard wouldn't. Perhaps it was business stress; maybe he *was* impotent and didn't want to admit it. Underneath his pleasant exterior he's tough and likes to think he's macho. Whatever, it just all got too much and then I met Alan."

"He was already in Sydney and came home for some family meeting or reunion. This was at the start of his new artistic career which held so much promise. He'd broken away from Wilga and her overpowering influence, so he was fun to be with. One thing led to another and eventually - well quite quickly really - I left Richard and came here to live with Alan. I divorced, we married and now here we are."

"How did you meet the Melville's? The modelling story obviously isn't true."

Monica's eyes twinkled mischievously.

"It wasn't entirely untrue either. I did model for Alan before and after we were married but I met the Melville's through work. I was an office temp."

"So you worked for them, caught the boss's eye -"

"Not very original but there you go."

"So what now?"

"Maybe legal action. I'll have to think about it. Would you like to stay for dinner?"

"I was going to ask you out. There must be plenty of good restaurants around here."

"There are and we've plenty of time."

Monica moved closer as she spoke, reaching and collecting the empty stubbie which Order heaved himself from the chair to hand to her. His hands free he put them to her shoulders and kissed the soft yielding lips.

"I'll get rid of these," Monica said quietly. "Won't be long."

However she was. Order heard a toilet flush and then a door open or close, all the while seeking to occupy himself in this relatively impersonal room without seeking to pry.

It was possible for Monica the hairdresser, according to Wilga, to become Monica the office temp according to Monica and the difference put down to some peculiar snobbery. On the other hand …

Monica's head and a bare shoulder appeared around the door. Her blue eyes sparkled with good humour as she asked in her husky voice: "Is there something about the word Yes you have trouble understanding, John?"

FOURTEEN

"**S**o how was Sydney?"

"Tiring, Liz," Order said, preoccupied with sorting out two days' accumulated mail and reliving two nights' memories. "What's been happening here?"

"Nothing I couldn't handle, but you've an urgent extra committee ..."

Order stopped listening. He was back in Sydney, that vital vibrant and beautiful metropolis upon the shimmering harbour. A place where he could not afford to live yet hated to leave. Monica made it more of a wrench now, so that the bland southern tablelands drive and the sun baked kilometres though ugly western Sydney suburbia before reaching her cosmopolitan territory almost made the journey worthwhile.

Almost, because Order was not fooling himself. Monica was a good enough lay and they had agreed to see more of each other, but three hours drive each way precluded too much regular intimacy and there was no sense in encouraging her to return to Canberra. He didn't want any permanent arrangement at this stage of his career and certainly not one associated with the locally influential Melville's.

Selfish as it was, he could not see Monica raising objections either, she didn't strike him as the type to simply accept what others wanted of her, not if Richard and Alan were anything to go by.

And he knew he still would have to be discreet about the relationship and having Monica remain in Sydney greatly helped the situation.

Such a liaison was not uncommon. There were plenty of public servants and consultants who lived and worked in Canberra during the week and went home to their families in the eastern state capitals at weekends. Some of these long distance commuters had local lovers and if their legally wedded spouses had any sense they either ignored thoughts of such extramarital goings-on or set up their own.

Nevertheless, they were not politicians and while the media might respect the private lives of elected representatives unless their behaviour became too blatant, the same could not be said for the party apparatchiks.

The party brass would be very alarmed if they knew Order was sleeping with the ex-wife of two of the Melville sons. Although Bernie never would reveal to an elected member the amount of a political donation or indeed the name of the donor - 'need to know basis, we don't want you being influenced by cheque books' - Order guessed the Melville's were big time contributors to election funds.

Even if they prudently paid into both government and opposition war chests, Bernie would not want the party's share threatened by a personal indiscretion. Pre-selection, the ultimate political sanction, could be decided upon such a lapse.

Thoughts of money reminded him of a question which had nagged his drive back from Sydney.

"Gabby? John Order. The Todd murder -"

"Suicide."

"Whatever. I'm wondering how secure a business empire is. Moby Investments it's called. Seems the late Alan Todd was here to get his share of it."

"How d'you know this?"

Order explained what Wilga and Monica had told him, although he did not tell the police officer of the different purpose they each ascribed to Alan's need for the money.

"Possible motive if it wasn't suicide," Gabby ruminated.

It wasn't and it is, Order thought, but he said: "Can we find out Moby's solvency?"

"I'll see," said the policeman, leaving Order unsure whether it could be done or should be done.

He wondered if he also should approach Phillip Keane, the opposition's business and consumer affairs spokesman and decided against doing so. He didn't know the man very well and, ever sensitive to treading upon someone else's political turf, guessed the inquiry could be misunderstood. It might even unjustifiably damage Moby Investments' financial standing if Keane lived up to his name.

Instead, Order decided to pump his friend, Rob Glasson, party business liaison task force member and deputy chair of the legislature's Planning Committee.

"I know the Melville's by reputation," Glasson confirmed over lunch, biting into a chicken sandwich, "an' the Galaxy business has come up in committee."

"Planning," he added, anticipating Order's question. "They're trying to obtain approvals for several more restaurants."

"Including Area Three where there's some opposition," said Order, remembering the recent public meeting.

"There's always opposition to any change in this city, John. The biggest collection of know-it-all whingers in the country live in Canberra. Everyone's an expert on something."

Order didn't argue. With its centers' of learning and of power, its military and political establishments, its government departments and attached high tech consultancies, Canberra probably had more per capita knowledge than anywhere else in the world since ancient Greece.

The situation was compounded by the city's annual climate of four distinct seasons, good medical and nursing home facilities, easy reach of Sydney and Melbourne, the south coast beaches and the Snowy Mountains' ski fields. An ideal place to retire,

Thus adding several generations of superannuated experts on something to the existing working experts on something.

All usually with insufficient interests to keep themselves occupied.

"And?"

"Hard to say. Objectors have nothing new to put forward. Noise, traffic and parking - the usual standbys - but the Government's nervous twelve month's from an election."

"If that," qualified Order, feeling guilty about his neglected door knocking. "Why is the Planning Committee involved?"

"Minor lease variation. Zoned commercial, not retail. Bloody bureaucrats."

Order wondered if the anger was directed at the public servants who had made this particular troublesome zoning decision or their predecessors who long ago decided planning issues in general were far too hot for them to handle and skillfully passed the job to a committee of politicians.

"Doesn't appear the Melville's have any money troubles if they want more restaurants?"

"You wouldn't think so. Unless they need more Galaxies to stay afloat?" Rob Glasson wondered aloud. "The Planning Committee can't help you there, John; it's outside our terms of reference."

FIFTEEN

Order spent the next few days attending to electoral correspondence, chasing up outstanding replies from ministers and, over the weekend, manning a shopping centre stall on the Saturday morning and door knocking in the afternoon.

Door knocking, like telephone polling, was something only the very insensitive enjoyed in Order's opinion. Personally, he found both activities intrusive and was pleased and grateful at the tolerance most people showed him for his unannounced invasion of their privacy.

Mothers with crying babies, old men doubled over walking sticks, pretty barefoot young women, macho young men smoking cigarettes, ethnic families who did not understand a word and children who regarded him with wide disbelieving eyes, all patiently listened to his spiel and generously accepted his calling card.

Order dutifully plodded around the suburban streets, clipboard ready to note the occasional complaint about long grass needing to be cut, speeding traffic or the lack of pre-school places nearby. Most people seemed relaxed about government services, the Betty Downer's a tiny minority, but Order still found the absent resident the most satisfying.

Sorry I missed you, he would scrawl across his card in red texta and place it out of sight under the front door. Always under the front door, Bernie insisted, because the letterbox raised doubts you really had bothered to walk to the house. Always out of sight, Bernie also insisted, so you didn't tip off undesirables the occupants might be out - and anger the occupants by advertising their absence.

The second most satisfying happening with door knocking was finishing for the day and sitting down somewhere with a cold beer and a virtuous feeling.

Which was when Monica telephoned late Sunday afternoon to say she was coming to Canberra in two days and could he pick her up from the bus station?

"I thought I should make another, well personal, approach to the Melville's," Monica said as they lay in her motel bed that night, "and if that doesn't work, I'll see about legal action."

Drowsy after their love making, Order struggled to concentrate. "Need any help?"

"No, I'll try to get Richard by himself, see if I can work through him to Wilga."

"You're still friends?" Because his own experience had been similar.

"I'd like to think so. It wasn't as if we hated each other. Just incompatible, I suppose."

"I'll try Richard tomorrow," Monica continued, "then I can see about lawyers if it doesn't work out."

"Local lawyers?"

"Of course. The Melville's have status in Canberra, in case you haven't noticed. The more embarrassment I can cause them locally, or threaten to do so, the better my chances of getting Alan's money."

"I hope you won't be disappointed about his share."

Order explained the enquiries he had initiated with the police to establish a possible motive for the murder of Alan Todd.

"I'll keep you informed," he murmured into Monica's ear.

"You'd better. I'm here for several days - and nights - and I don't go to sleep early, so if you are out at boring meetings you can still call me if you want to come over and brief me." She gestured to the night table. "I've brought the mobile this trip."

Pulling up the sheet to take the edge off the air-conditioning, Order made a mental note to take the machine's number before he eventually wearily headed for home, grateful the House was not sitting this week.

He was trying to appear interested in updating the monthly diary, crosschecking with the separate records Liz kept, when Gabby Williams telephoned.

"No bad vibes about the Melville's businesses," he told Order, "the expansion plan for the Galaxy restaurants is financially okay an' they're cashed up."

"Even if Todd had pulled out his share?"

"Can't say. We don't know what his share would have been - an' I can't get that sort of information. Melville's companies are all private not public."

Not getting far there, Order thought, after thanking the policeman and hanging up.

Turning back to the unexciting task of pencilling in appointments, he decided Monica would have to take the expensive legal road if she was to obtain financial justice.

SIXTEEN

Order attended a local branch meeting the evening of Gabby's telephone call so it was after ten when he contacted Monica to say he was coming to the motel.

The meeting had left him edgy, the fault of one man: Bob Bennett. Bob and his wife, Lorraine, were no friends of Order, who had beaten the aforesaid Bob in the preselection as candidate for the seat he subsequently had won in the by-election.

Ever since, Bennett took every opportunity to question, to argue with and, if possible, to embarrass Order at party meetings. The attempted white-anting was obvious to all and Bernie had told Order Bob Bennett was doing himself more damage in the eyes of the rank and file than he could ever do to him.

Nevertheless, the constant attacks irritated Order, particularly when Bennett used the branch meetings' question times to make him seem ignorant of local issues.

"You can't know everything, John," Bernie counselled him. "Just plant a few questions among your friends which you *can* answer."

In spite of Bernie's assurances, Order thought it wise to stay chatting over coffee until Bennett had gone home.

"Sorry I'm late," he spoke into his hands-free mobile as he backed out of the club's parking lot. "You said I could come over anytime."

"Yes, of course. Where are you now?" Monica sounded distracted.

"About ten minutes away."

"Oh. Ten minutes away," she repeated, stupidly he thought.

"Something the matter?"

"No. Nothing, John. See you soon."

Monica's welcome was warmer when he arrived in her room. The motel car park had been inactive and inside the unit nothing, least of all the bed, was disturbed so he dismissed the doubt in his mind Monica hadn't been alone when he telephoned her.

"Why d'you want me to 'phone ahead?" he asked, as one last try.

"So I can be ready when you arrive," she said huskily and, putting her arms around his neck, asked: "Coffee? It's just boiled."

"So you're going to have to take the legal road," he said much later, stroking the blonde hair highlighted by moonlight in the darkened room. "Need a good one?"

"I'll be okay for the moment. I'd like to talk to the family's solicitors first. Maybe that way we can avoid nasty publicity."

"As far as I know," Monica continued when Order remained silent, "nobody has associated Alan's death, suicide, with the Melville's. Am I right?"

"Nothing from the local media that I've seen, Monica."

"So much for investigative journalism."

"Well he did have a different name," Order began but without much conviction because he knew she was right. Even the parliamentary media gallery these days worked exclusively off releases issued by politicians.

"Which gives me a lever," Monica interrupted, raising herself on one elbow and looking down upon Order in the darkened bed. "The Melville's are a completely amoral family, they have no thought for what's right or wrong, only that they can attain their aims."

"Of money, it seems."

"And status, John. Remember?" she exclaimed. "That's where they're vulnerable now."

"The Melville's have worked hard, built up their interests from nothing. Old Melville was a brickie or a carpenter when he first came here in the '80's to work on the new Parliament House, or so he said -"

"You knew him?"

"A bit. He was pretty much a drunk toward the end. Who wouldn't be with Wilga for a wife? And that's something else, she was a bank teller or something when they got together and got lucky."

"Howso?"

"After the permanent parliament house was built there were lots of men who had been employed on the building now looking for a job and the government started releasing land for housing to keep them occupied, the unions happy and to satisfy the consumer demands of the growing national capital. Melville began working in this field and then decided to upgrade from an employee to a sub-contractor then to a contractor. The rest is history, as they say."

Order knew the story was true. Canberra had provided so many of its wealthy citizens with just such an opportunity to make good after unremarkable beginnings in dusty dying country towns or the anonymous jungles of the bigger coastal cities. Melville's climb was not unusual; plenty of efficient and ambitious tradesmen formed their own businesses in the good times. Where Melville *was* unusual was that he had survived where most of the other ambitious artisans went back to working for a wage when the always fragile, cyclical local building booms went bust.

It took hard work, strong nerves and guts to succeed in those cutthroat circumstances and Order reminded himself again the Melville's were not to be underestimated.

"Now they've made it, they're looking for social acceptance?" he asked the shadowy ceiling.

Monica's voice sounded triumphant.

"Exactly, John."

"The last thing they'd want would be a scandal involving a dead son in mysterious circumstances and a public brawl over his share of the estate, never mind how old Melville tied it up."

Order remembered with a touch of sadness for his hosts, the Melville barbeque, attended only by their employees, and even the earlier cocktail party and the quick way Dick Melville had been palmed off onto him. No, they hadn't achieved the status they craved yet and Todd's death would be a long-term serious setback to such aspirations.

"I think it's your best shot, Monica," Order decided, reaching for her again, "but I wouldn't leave it too long."

She snuggled against him.

"I don't intend to, but why?"

"Because I think there'll be further developments. The Downer woman saw Richard or Terry or someone very like them leaving the property after Alan died and I'm reasonably confident I can reinterest the police in my theory that it wasn't suicide."

Monica was quick to react, sitting up suddenly and speaking appealingly.

"Give me the rest of my stay here, would you, John? I'm broke remember? I'll need to get some firm undertaking before the plods turn up."

"It may not help your case. Probably the estate share will be frozen pending the police investigation – it is a motive – and if it is murder you might be waiting years."

"I'll have to take that chance. I'll go for something in writing. Please don't cramp my attempt until I've tried this visit."

"Monday. I'll give you until Monday. I can't delay speaking to the police any longer than then."

"Monday will be fine," Monica murmured into his ear, her hands busy. "That's enough time without being urgent - unlike now."

SEVENTEEN

Thursday was a bad day.

It began driving to the Post Office, with Order, late for an appointment having overslept, held up in peak hour traffic by someone ahead who insisted on driving below the speed limit. Canberra was a city where most people knew their rights but not always their responsibilities.

He could not find a park outside the building and when he finally reached it he noticed the entire five minute zone parking bays taken up with drivers opening and reading their mail, like children who can't wait to open presents.

Hot and thoroughly out-of-sorts Order arrived at the office to learn he need not have hurried, the constituent was a no-show, simply had not turned up for the appointment which yesterday had been so urgent.

He didn't have the courage to complain to Liz. She always was at him to make more use of his mobile to stay in touch with the office. Anyway, she had other matters to report on.

"Mrs. Downer's been on the 'phone again about the fence and can you sit in on the AID's Select Committee for half an hour at two o'clock for Julie Davenport?"

"Why me?"

"She's double booked herself. It's only thirty minutes - needs to pick up the kids from somewhere, I think. Working mothers' syndrome."

The AID's Select Committee was going nowhere and a waste of time. Set up by the Government to silence gay community complaints about inaction following a local resurgence in the disease, it was a calculated exercise in political correctness, reflected in the neat balance of pushy women and wimpish men forming the membership. Most of the male politicians hated it.

"I can't vote," Order warned.

"She knows that, John. There won't be a vote anyway, they're only interviewing witnesses. The committee's agreed to you sitting in."

Under Standing Orders any member could, with the approval of a committee's elected members, attend the public meetings of that committee. With permission they could even ask questions but they could not vote. This type of substitution was a sneaky way to take a break from the boredom of committee work and Order firmly believed, Julie Davenport accepted, the only people who wanted to sit through an all day public committee hearing were the departmental spies or recorders as they were more euphemistically known.

His bad hair day continued when Julie did not turn up until the tea break at three fifteen.

"Sorry, John. Took longer than I thought," she said unconvincingly.

Order shrugged. "I don't know why you wanted me, Julie. Finlay was there."

"The quorum was safe, of course, but Finn's usually half-asleep after lunch. Anyway, thanks again."

"You owe me," Order said with a grim smile.

Julie Davenport paused at the door to the room where the committee was reconvening.

"Yes I do and I'll pay now. Word's out you've been spending late late nights at the Stardust Motel. See yah."

"Bernie called. Would you 'phone him?" Liz asked when he returned to the office.

Order thought uneasily of the balding, cardigan-wearing heavy smoker who had one of the best political brains in this city of politics and who didn't contact politicians unnecessarily.

"You're private life's your own, John," Bernie was not one for nice preliminaries, "but the walls have ears in Canberra."

"I'm single, Bernie."

"I'm not worried about the news media; it's the gossip columnists who might pick up on it. She's an attractive blonde, I believe. Of course," he added, "if it's serious then there's nothing to worry about."

Order paused in his response. He hadn't told Bernie any of his suspicions about Alan Todd's death and the probable involvement of the party-backing Melville's. He hadn't thought much about his feelings for Monica either, save at a very superficial level.

"I'm not sure about that yet," he said truthfully.

"It's your business, John. You just need to know it's been noticed. 'Bye."

So what, Order decided as he replaced the receiver with careful deliberation. We're both adults, not married nor in any other way encumbered. Monica's not a constituent and I'm simply helping her obtain financial justice.

None of which dispelled the nagging worry of what public exposure of their real association could do to his political career.

There was a significant body of wowsers in Canberra. The Catholic Right, many of the WASP's and, increasingly, the supporters of fundamentalist religions whose members seemed to be growing by the week.

And wowsers were not confined to the churches or the conservatives.

Feminists, environmentalists and ethic groups all at one time or another came out in support of this dry and bitter lifestyle and Order knew many individual voters of this disparate collection of spoilsports supported his Party and by association, him.

He also knew they did not easily forgive.

"Don't forget you're addressing the Women's Institute tonight," Liz reminded him when he told her he was going out.

Order was unsure why he was going to see Monica unannounced and in daylight. Perhaps it was some defiant urge to demonstrate he had nothing to hide.

Nevertheless, discretion led him to seek out the visitor's car park rather than the bay reserved in front of the unit for Monica's vehicle had she had one.

He need not have troubled himself. The slot already was occupied by a battered yellow Toyota Order was sure he had seen somewhere before.

As he watched, Monica's door opened and Mrs. Boone said her goodbyes to someone out-of-sight.

"Why didn't you tell me?"

"You seem to be asking me that question a lot lately, John."

She'd resumed her seat on one of the two chairs at the occasional table. Order still stood fighting to control his anger, which had been building after parking the car and quickly making his way to the motel room.

"I didn't want Avril involved. She's an old school friend who's doing it tough. I thought the money might help - Alan said he'd pay board - then he died. I'm not handling this very well, am I?" she concluded with a sad smile.

"What was she doing here if you didn't want her involved?"

"Alan didn't pay," Monica understated patiently. "Avril has a car, which you know I don't, so she called 'round to collect."

"So you 'phoned her?"

"Of course I 'phoned her," Monica said, exasperated. "She's my friend and we owed her money."

"Okay. Forget it." He pulled out the second chair and sat down. "Any progress with the Melville's?"

"I'm waiting for a 'phone call," she said, her hands reaching for his own.

It was later, driving back to the office, he realised with a stab of delight - desire being temporarily satisfied - Monica hadn't been in the least angry at his unannounced visit.

EIGHTEEN

The Women's Institute met in one of Canberra's many social clubs, a feature of the city which amazed most citizens who could not understand how each of these staunchly independent organisations stayed solvent.

The majority of them had begun as ethnic or sporting watering holes for the faithful.

As succeeding generations became assimilated, the old ethnic bonds weakened and the advent of the breathalyser and a nominated driver killed off the celebrations or wakes of most convivial post-sporting gatherings.

Nannyville-on-the-Molonglo, Order had heard Canberra described with regret by many smoking, drinking old-timers.

The room was tatty, once fashionable cheap straight backed chairs were lined up in largely empty rows, particularly at the front - a common aversion at any public meeting save for the bottoms of invited guests.

What the audience lacked in numbers they more than made up for in cordiality and Order's address was well received.

Over supper Lorraine Bennett approached him.

"I hear you've got yourself a regular out-of-town girlfriend, John?"

As the president of the Institute discretely moved away, Order accepted the challenge.

"Out-of-town constituent really, Lorraine. Obviously with a local issue to resolve."

"Well, the Melville's will take some resolving. They're good Party supporters so I hope you can handle it."

Later, moving through the almost empty designated poker machine room, with garish *No Smoking* stickers upon every bandit, Order wondered how his political enemies also had found out about Monica.

Inspecting overgrown damp drainage ditches was not his first choice for the morning's priorities. However, the constituent was off to Sydney on an early flight and wanted the problem examined as soon as possible.

Order was drying out the cuffs of his trousers while reading the newspaper, the list of forthcoming events and the day's appointments upon the desk before him in neat computer-type, when the press photograph caught his eye.

Galaxy bouncer in Court on assault charge. Youth groups demonstrate against brutal attack upon public art exponent, Order read.

Squarely in the photographer's lens, surrounded by angry graffiti supporters, was the Melville's Gonzo.

His telephone call to Gabby Williams was not returned until after visits of a small supermarket owner who wanted No Stopping signs removed from behind his shop so deliveries could be made and a scruffy suit who sought substantial compensation from the government for the wrongful arrest of his now dead father in an anti-Vietnam protest decades ago.

"I'll make enquiries, John," Williams said with the resignation of one who has to humour elected representatives. "He doesn't fit your profile 'though."

"Mrs. Downer's, not mine. An' she's old and only saw the man from a distance."

"I'll check."

Order's telephone call to the Stardust was not answered so lunch was off. Nevertheless, it set him thinking about Monica and her truthfulness.

"She certainly hasn't been honest with me," he confided to Rob Glasson, over toasted sandwiches and coffee in up market Manuka. "But each time I confront her with it, she has a plausible explanation."

"Her friend had a car, her ex didn't pay the rent, and she needed someone to be an intermediary with the Melville's. It is all plausible, isn't it?"

"Listen mate," Glasson wiped the chocolate from his lips. "You're making a new boy's fundamental political mistake. Don't get personally involved. This woman's asked for your help with some constituents. Okay, very powerful one's, which is all the more reason to just do what you can as a good local member an' don't get involved further."

"Well I am."

"Christ, you're not screwing her?"

"I mean the suspicions - my suspicions - about her husband's death not being suicide." He decided to risk it: "There's a filthy rumour around about Monica and me."

"I've heard. Your friends the Bennett's. Be careful, John, they'll spread it all through your branches an' your conservative supporters won't like it."

"I know."

But Order really wondered how the Bennett's, Bernie and everyone else had come to know.

* * *

Monica made no contact over the weekend and Order's telephone calls to the motel and to the mobile were unanswered.

Not that he was bored. Shopping for a few basic items and attending two fetes - quick look-ins where he purchased raffle tickets and hoped someone recognised him - filled Saturday morning, with door knocking in the afternoon.

Saturday night he was present at a big ethnic gathering outside the electorate along with most other members of the parliament.

"Politicians have to suck up to ethnic groups because our political masters believe they vote as a block," Bernie once explained to him. "Funny outcome from decades of multiculturalism and integration, don't you think?"

Order envied the members who had given apologies, being otherwise engaged, and those who had accepted and then didn't show up - it was a large enough function for this rudeness not to be noticed. Infuriatingly, both absent groups were acknowledged.

"It really pisses me off," grumbled Tim Forbes during a break in the formalities. "Those bastards had no intention of being here, yet they're getting the same billing as those of us who are here."

"But at least we're seen."

"An' that's all, kiddo. You won't get any more benefit from tonight an' it's not worth the effort. Who's going to remember you were present as opposed to being mentioned? It comes down to name recognition, that's all, not whether you're here in the flesh."

Order did not have the chance of confirming his more experienced colleague's observation until supper.

This was some time off as spokesman after spokesman - and nary a woman - delighted to have as a captive audience such influential community leaders, seized the opportunity to address them at length.

"How many provinces does this shitty country have, John?" asked Tim imploringly, as a fourth speaker began a new regional tour of his ancestral homeland.

"They're not really interested in us, y'know," Rob Glasson said as the three politicians later stood together near the bar.

"Shouldn't we join them? Mix a bit?"

"You can try," said Forbes, "but it's my experience they prefer their own friends' company an' in their own language. They'll be polite, of course, speak English, smile, introduce you, but it won't last long an' the group will gradually, quietly, break up."

"Then why are we here?"

"Status, I think," Glasson expertly intercepted a drink waiter as he spoke.

"Bit pointless, isn't it?"

"Too right. You end up driven to attend these events, John. You feel guilty if you're home Saturday night with your feet up when you could, even should, be out in the electorate."

"Bloody time wasting as many of them are," Forbes joined in, "you don't want to get tossed out at the next election just because you didn't attend important functions."

"So we put up with it?" Order asked, pushing away the ever present spectre of electoral defeat.

"Yes an' no, John," Forbes continued. "At least as far as I'm concerned."

"He's talking about his lemon list," Glasson interrupted.

"My list of annual functions which are so bloody terrible I won't attend again. I call them lemons because they suck and make me pull a face if ever I remember them."

"Easier for you with a very safe seat, Tim," Glasson said enviously. "I think I'll head off before I become a candidate for booze bus attention."

"Me too," agreed Forbes. "No way the police spokesman can risk getting caught driving over the limit. See yah."

Order looked around the happy chattering crowd, relaxed in friendly groups, and realised his friends were right, there was no place for him in these companionable circles.

Not seeing any other politicians, he was moving toward the exit door when a voice called a greeting.

"Mr. Order. How nice to see you here. I would've thought you had far more enjoyable things to do on this Saturday night than attend an unexciting function?"

Wilga Melville smiled winked and moved majestically back into the crowd.

NINETEEN

School holidays always resulted in a change to the parliament's sitting pattern. Democracy's small recognition its defenders led other lives, as Bernie put it, so the House had another non-sitting week to allow legislators' to re-introduce themselves to their children and the family dog.

None of which directly concerned John Order.

Thus Monday began a week of committee meetings, constituent visits and on Wednesday an overnight in Melbourne for a private testimonial dinner.

Monica remained out of touch and Order was reluctant to tell Gabby Williams of his suspicions until he had spoken to her, so the agreed deadline before he advised the policeman passed.

Williams did contact him but he had little new to divulge.

"Your Gonzo is an interesting fellow, John, even though he doesn't fit the profile you're trying to create."

"Howso?"

"Gonzo or the profile?" the inspector asked, then abruptly: "No matter, enquiries continuing."

Order hardly had time to ponder these enigmatic remarks before Liz told him Terry Melville was on the telephone.

"I'm in Sydney but I'll be back Friday. How about lunch?"

They met at an outdoor Kingston restaurant with unsteady chairs and circular tables comfortably accommodating only two lattes and small main courses. Around them sat tall thin attractive young women in dark business attire. The emphasis was on pants suits.

"They look like they'd eat you up," Terry observed nastily, nodding around him, "but they're not so hot. Half of them are worried about their kid in child care somewhere an' the other half if they'll ever get around to having one. You married?"

"Once. Briefly."

"When you were a politician?"

"No." And be thankful for the small mercy.

"So what d'you do for entertainment? Canberra's a great place to raise spoilt children, but there's not much on offer to a forty something single. That's why I prefer Sydney."

Order looked across at Terry Melville as the man spoke, noting again the thickening moustache and the World War II glamour boy appeal.

"I don't get much time for that."

"Not what I've been hearing, John, even if she is an import. Alan's widow, Monica, isn't it?"

The arrival and the maneuverings to table place the Caesar salads gave Order time to prepare a reply.

"I wondered what this lunch was for," he began with a smile. "Has she seen your mother yet, because that's what Monica Todd asked me to try to arrange?"

"No idea. As I told you, I've been in Sydney all week an' don't feel your privacy has been invaded, John. I couldn't give a rat's whether or not you and Monica *are* a horizontal item. Anyway, why does she want to see Wilga?"

"Don't like her chances," Terry opined, stroking his moustache gently as Order finished the explanation. "There's no obligation, you see, to look after Monica. Alan would have been a different case."

"Howso?"

"Well, as family he was entitled to a share of my father's estate."

"And he came here to get it."

"Who said? Monica? Yes, it would have to be Monica,' Terry

decided, "an' nobody can disprove her because Alan's dead."

"D'you think it was suicide?" Order asked quietly.

"Jesus, what else could it be? Are you suggesting somebody killed him?"

"There's a motive."

"My mad brother's share of the estate, you mean? Let me tell you Moby Investments is well enough financially to allow Alan to take his share an' go."

"Then why not give it to Monica - or at least some of it?"

"Doesn't work that way with the Melville's. You have to be born into the money. Marrying in isn't enough."

"Not even twice?" Order said teasingly.

"What's this twice?" Terry was genuinely mystified.

"Why Monica …"

"And Richard and Alan," completed Terry. 'Jesus, she's still trotting out that old canard. Look, Monica did marry Alan right enough, but it was only after she'd been Richard's girlfriend, mistress and playmate an' maybe the old man's as well."

"So there was no problem about Richard being dominated by Wilga, therefore destroying the marriage?"

"There *was* no marriage! Could you see Monica ditching Richard if she was his lawful wedded to take a chance on poor mad Alan?"

"She said she loved him. Alan, that is."

Order, bewildered at the turn of the conversation, tried to recall her words.

"I don't think you're bedding Monica," Terry decided, "because you certainly don't know her very well."

"She's a gold-digger, John," Terry Melville's eyes expressed pity at the gullibility of the man opposite. "Having landed Richard she'd have held on. No, the best she could do was Alan, but she didn't anticipate him killing himself."

"And the frustrated artist?"

"Fantasy. Alan was a drunk like the old man an' he also did low risk drugs like pot. What he didn't do was an honest day's work. Ever."

"Sydney?"

"Oh Sydney's correct, but not in search of the bohemian life. Alan was packed off there, a remittance man they used to be called, to get him out of our hair in Canberra. The Melville's have a reputation to protect an' too much has gone into establishing it to have it threatened by a weak link in the family chain."

There was no false modesty in Terry's words.

"We even roped Monica into the scheme. The business would pay them a generous monthly allowance if they'd stay away from Canberra. It was Monica's job to make sure that that happened."

"Probably explains why she thinks you owe her," Order suggested.

"We don't owe her a cent. She broke her contract. She let Alan come back here."

"But why?"

"Who knows? He's dead."

"Perhaps Monica knows?"

"She hasn't said anything yet, has she? To you, I mean?" Terry grinned. "Nobody else has seen her as far as I'm aware."

A strange buzzing noise forestalled Order's reply.

"Excuse me. Yes?" Terry withdrew a mobile telephone from his coat pocket, turning away as he did so.

Order was training himself to use his mobile more often but he still couldn't shake off the old fashioned privacy a telephone booth provided. Airport lounges were the worst, with suits of both sexes talking seriously to the office Order suspected they had only recently left, telling the world as well if it wanted to listen in to the conversation.

"I'll have to get back to you," Terry said, adding hurriedly, "I'm having lunch with John Order."

"Now where were we?" Terry tucked the mobile away as he spoke. "This theory of yours, well maybe suspicion. Told anyone yet? Monica? Police?"

"I promised Monica I'd let her speak to Wilga before I told the police everything."

"Why?"

"Well, if she came to a financial arrangement it doesn't matter much how he died. There's no longer a motive, so no grounds for the law to pursue enquiries."

"Don't build your hopes. Wilga's not likely to feel generous. Anyway, what's this everything you can tell the police?"

"They discount my suspicions but I've now a witness who saw a man in the backyard of the house where Alan died at about the same time. Carrying a golf bag. Looked a bit like you, Terry."

"That's not very funny, Order. I don't play golf, shooting is my sport, an' I wasn't within miles of Alan." The confidence he had brought to the meeting became aggressive.

"Really?"

"As far as I can recall I was at home an' if so, there'll be plenty of witnesses. Now if you don't mind, I'd better be shoving off."

And that thought Order at the wheel, waiting for people quietly enjoying their power to hold up traffic ambling across a pedestrian crossing that was interesting.

That being the verbal chameleon which was Monica's story-telling and then the lunchtime telephone conversation of a doubtlessly busy important businessman.

Because only somebody they both knew would understand Terry's simple reference to new boy John Order when speaking on his mobile 'phone.

TWENTY

"**W**here have you been?"

It was late Friday afternoon and the parliamentary office wing was largely in darkness, no welcoming light from most doorways now securely locked for the weekend.

"Sydney. I thought you'd have guessed," Monica said angrily, irritated perhaps at having to explain such an obvious answer.

"Seen Wilga yet?"

"What chance have I had? Have you spoken to the police?"

"I waited to hear from you."

"I'm sorry to have mucked you around, John," her tone softened, "an' now I'm going to do so again, by asking for more time."

"Say another week?" she pleaded.

"Why not? The situation's the same now or in seven day's time."

"Well, say Monday week?"

"Okay. Anyway, where are you?"

"Jolimont bus station. Can't you hear the noise?"

"I'll be there in ten minutes," said Order emphatically, replacing the receiver before she could object.

"Motel or mine?" he asked, as Monica buckled into the seat belt.

"Motel. I don't want to compromise you too much," she said, squeezing his thigh.

"Compromise? Most of *my* Canberra seems to know all about us already."

"D'you mind?" Hesitantly.

"Not really. People only care if you're double dipping - an' half of them are simply jealous. What took you down to Sydney?"

"Alan's place. The agent wanted it cleared out so they could let it again. I couldn't see the point of paying more rent but clearing it took longer than I thought."

Once more a plausible explanation, with Monica going on to say there was no telephone - long since disconnected - her mobile's battery was flat and she had been too busy to seek out a rare public telephone box.

Order thought of asking about Richard and Alan and Monica's marital status but it seemed superfluous with one dead and the other out of the picture.

It was over a late dinner Monica revisited the extra week she'd negotiated earlier.

"D'you think we could make it a fortnight?"

"Why so long?"

"Just insurance. I don't want to be asking you for more and more time, it's humiliating an' surely the police can wait a little longer?"

True, he thought, Todd's not going anywhere further.

"Anyway, the following week's a holiday Monday," Monica pressed on more confidently, "so I've got to tie it up by then."

Monday public holidays were tiresome, disrupting Order's orderly routine and generally presaging three long empty days. Few organisations planned activities over a long weekend when most of Canberra took the easy two hour drive to the New South Wales south coast. .

"Howso?"

"The Melville's generally go away weekends, certainly long weekends, according to Alan, so there is no hope of seeing them then. And I can't be away from work much longer. This fortnight is my last shot, although I hope to settle it once and for all this next week."

"And then?" Order said quietly, feeling randy again.

"Depends upon the result. Or will you ditch me if I loose the Melville millions?" Monica shoeless beneath the table stroked a foot higher and higher against Order's right inside leg.

"That needs to be - no! Let's wait an' see."

Order moved back from the table, the better to protect himself.

"Careful. I'm a public figure."

"So let's go back to the motel." Monica resumed her foot work, ankle level.

"Suits me. I can't wait, only I don't want it to be so obvious, here in this restaurant."

"Then you leave first, I'll follow later. Don't stick me with the bill, though."

"I can't do that. Looks like we've had a fight."

"I'll go to the toilet then an' you can wait."

"How about you just go. With your foot massage I'm not able to go anywhere at present," Order whispered, remembering teenage embarrassment in public places.

"Here, take the car keys."

"I assumed you didn't want me to drive?" Monica asked from the passenger seat when he finally arrived after a needed toilet stop. "I don't, by the way."

Which explains why everyone comes to you, Order decided much later as he headed for home, faced with the prospect of a wearying weekend.

He was door knocking tomorrow afternoon and attending a charity auction tomorrow night, which he probably could escape by eleven. Sunday morning was a door knocking no-no, because people liked to sleep in, play with the children or make them and read the newspapers. Some even went to church.

However, Sunday afternoon was a door knock imperative and although the evening was free open restaurants were not easy to find on Sunday night in the cosmopolitan national capital.

He was now in Civic and Canberra's central nightclub strip

along Northbourne Avenue was humming. Teenagers and yuppies milled around outside the popular bars, vehicles cruised in the curb side lane looking for action and God knows how many illegal drugs in whatever form were being negotiated in cash or kind under the Spanish colonnades of East and West Row.

Road rage was understandable, Order conceded, when the vehicle in front of him at the traffic lights put out a right turning blinker only when the lights changed to green.

Unsurprised, he noted it was ACT registered and not a tourist.

Held up while the selfish local made a leisurely turn, Order's attention was attracted by a luminous sign in the rear window of the Pajero ahead of him in the centre lane.

Baby On Board, it claimed, whether as a warning to other drivers as to possible unpredictability by the person at the wheel in the event of some baby-like crisis or simply as a boast that we've done it, Order never could work out. Not for a moment did he imagine the sign was an extra caution to other motorists to exercise care when approaching the now baby mobile from behind.

It was liberating to be free of Civic and its young hormone-driven desires and expectations. Nevertheless, he did not let this petty freedom go to his head. The breath tests and speed checks in this most controlled of Australian cities posed a threat to all, but especially to a very junior public figure.

The yuppie 4WD driver obviously thought the same and had fallen behind, even well below Order's sedate but not attention attracting speed.

Driving onto the parkway he moved to the left hand lane, leaving the 4WD to overtake and presumably, get baby-on-board home speedily for more breastfeeding or whatever.

In doing so, the headlights picked up a wayside cross bedecked with flowers.

Over the past few decades these testaments to death on the road had become commonplace in multicultural Canberra, although why you would want to make a roadside shrine from a possible driving stupidity escaped him.

Indeed, in the more cynical political quarters these roadside memorials were known as DD's - Dickhead Deaths or more politely, Driver Distractions.

Steering off the parkway, Order noticed another vehicle had followed. Not a matter of concern until in the narrow one lane road lined with George Weston's longevity trees, the Pajero decided to overtake, too closely.

Order eased gently upon the foot brake but the 4WD moved ever closer, narrowing the gap to force his car onto the verge, down the embankment and into the densely planted thick tree trunks.

He felt rather than heard the first scrape as the heavier vehicle brushed against the sedan. If he could not be forced from the road then someone was determined to push him off.

There was no mistaking the intent. The second time he heard the scrape he saw the wing mirror beside him shatter and break away. Whoever this maniacal baby-birther was Order had no chance to see: it was too dark and he was white-knuckle driving to keep his car on the bitumen.

He had no choice. The nearest suburb was some distance ahead and oncoming traffic non-existent.

Order depressed the foot brake, hard.

The tires screamed, the bodywork took another bashing but the vehicle stopped, the rear end fishtailing alarmingly. The Pajero meanwhile, propelled by its own speed, shot past the now stationary sedan onto the verge and down the slope, bumping its way at an acute angle toward the trees.

Order didn't wait for the conclusion to what he hoped would be an ugly fiery accident. With the pungent smell of rubber coming through the air-conditioning vents, he drove off at high speed, wondering if the reason was simply unaccountable road rage or was it something more sinister?

TWENTY ONE

The parliamentary vehicle fleet liaison officer was not pleased.

"You should have stopped and exchanged licence details, Mr. Order, as the instruction manual requires. Looks like both of these panels will have to be replaced an' there's no paperwork to document the accident."

"It was dark an' I didn't fancy confronting a hoon - or hoons - on a lonely road," Order explained. "I went back on Saturday, but there was nothing except some tire marks on the slope. Must have driven out of the ditch."

"We'll need to assess the extent of the damage," she said gloomily. "Might have to write it off. You'll need another vehicle while we make the assessment, but it'll take a day to get one. Can you put up with this scarred bodywork for a day, Mr. Order? There's no mechanical or electrical problem as far as I can see - although you'll have to sign off absolving Fleet of any responsibility."

"Okay. Where do I sign?" Order asked, realising he'd be late for the party meeting.

His Friday night scrape - literally - had not been picked up by the media. Thus Order didn't have to read about a tired and emotional politician wrecking a taxpayer-funded vehicle nor subsequently face the euphemistically-free party room's quietly spread assessment that he was simply pissed out of his mind.

Order was grateful for the shared ignorance, because like an animal a politician was only safe if healthily clean. If an animal was sick, maimed or old, it no longer commanded the respect of its peers, its younger rivals nor its predators and, according to Bernie's gospel, so too went politicians.

"Nasty mess of your car," Rob Glasson murmured, sitting down beside him. "Saw you talking to Fleet."

"Shopping car parks in pay week become manic."

With a two week sitting ahead there was a significant lack of passion in Fearless Leader's comments. Or at least in Order's opinion. Maybe he was losing it.

There was the usual and probably still unsuccessful plea for members to pass to Mother Hubbard, the media relations section, details of all constituent contacts over the previous month.

The MRS then would pass these names, addresses and interests to a data bank run by the party machine. Named Constituency Concerns, the aim was to continue the never-ending quest to get into voters' minds, hearts and prejudices for their ultimate support at the ballot box.

Most members were distrustful of Constituency Concerns, which they abbreviated to The Con, believing it only was a way of taking supporters from individual politicians and Order, new as he was, agreed.

"I would like a commitment from each of you to provide a minimum of twenty constituency contacts per month," the Leader of the Opposition intoned, without seeking the promise.

An argument then broke out between supporters of the moderate wing and the hard Right as to the Party's approach to a law and order amendment. No decision was reached before the bells began ringing to summon members to the Chamber, so a hasty truce was brokered.

With the territory's self-government relatively new, the Chamber did not display the aged timber and historic scrollwork of its counterparts elsewhere in Australia. Indeed its severe functionality, the space between members' desks and the clear sightlines to public and politician alike, was often envied by visiting parliamentarians confined to a museum of discomfort in their own legislatures.

Not everything had changed however, and most people in the building enjoyed the pomp and ceremony of the now wigless Speaker's procession behind the Mace to open the day's proceedings. They even could tolerate the call for an unspoken prayer or reflection - the latter a nineties condescension to the power of political correctness.

Some of the older members such as Paul Serverin refused to be present for this break with tradition and would not be rostered for House duty at the commencement of the day's programme.

Order was not concerned one way or the other, taking his rostered turn when it came up. The matter of a roster was largely unnecessary anyway as there usually were enough members in the Chamber to make up the quorum - half of the members of the House plus one member - demanded to begin the day's proceedings.

His only reservation about being in the House at its daily beginning was getting caught up in a condolence motion.

Unless controlled condolence motions became a regurgitation of an increasingly larger-than-life person's career. At some point they also became a me-too exercise, with more and more members speaking and contributing little new material. In consequence, upon the death of well-known or important people both Whips to stem the talk fest usually offended many colleagues by denying them the opportunity to say anything.

So Order sat in his office wading through the lengthy recommendations of the Health Committee's enquiry into the incidence of *Chlamydia trachomatis* among ACT residents.

Health was not his area of responsibility or special interest and therefore he read only the recommendations and not the Report itself. This was normal practise among paper-swamped politicians, yet even this abbreviated resume showed how a level-headed committee of the parliament was able so easily to remove itself from financial reality and call for a blank cheque approach to correcting the problems its investigations uncovered. Little wonder most reports gathered dust in departmental basements.

With half an ear to the televised debate in the Chamber, currently a self-righteous homily from one of the smaller party's representatives, Order reached across to pick up his telephone receiver.

"Mrs. Melville. You in?"

"Okay. Put her through, Liz."

"And what are you doing for the long weekend, John?" Wilga asked after the briefest of pleasantries.

"Electoral work, probably doorknocking. Catching up on correspondence an' household chores."

He was not looking forward to the long weekend. Monica would be back in Sydney he supposed and doorknocking over a holiday weekend was largely a waste of effort with so many people away.

"You'll be wasting your time doorknocking," Wilga confirmed. 'So many away. Why don't you take some time off yourself? All work an' no play, y'know."

The Melvilles usually go away on holiday weekends, he remembered Monica saying.

"We've a property south of Canberra," said Wilga. "It's an easy two hour drive. Why don't you join us? Do some shooting. There are feral pigs in the bush."

"I don't shoot."

"Oh, pity. Anyway why not at least come down for lunch? Say Sunday?"

A break in routine, a run in the country, would be good for him, Order agreed, and replaced the receiver as the division bells began their impatient clamour.

"We're voting no," said the Whip as Order moved past him into the Chamber.

With the cross-bench members of the minor parties supporting the Government in all floor votes save the occasional procedural matter, the result was foregone.

"What happens if Harold isn't here one day?" Order had asked Rob Glasson.

"We all make bloody fools of ourselves an' we get a new Whip."

His question was asked in the very early days of Order's political apprenticeship when he genuinely tried to understand and to follow the debates in the Chamber.

Now. like most other members, he no longer listened to the steady monotone of the person on their feet. Occasionally, when the member paused for breath, Mr. Speaker Harris raised his eyes to see if they had sat down and it was time to call another member to contribute to the debate.

Otherwise Mr. Speaker's job was to silence the loud private conversations with which members replaced the politeness of listening to each other's predictable contributions.

Apart from these duties the Speaker often seemed comatose.

Question Time was the exception, the dramatic performance of each day which immediately followed the lunch break.

Then Mr. Speaker needed all of his wits and his command of the Standing Orders as the Chamber engaged in noisy verbal cut and thrust.

Here the Opposition lawyers showed off to the House, the web of their questions designed to trap an unwary Minister. Here Order discovered there were other members whose main contribution to parliamentary debate was to constantly interject upon the person speaking.

Here Order found the women parliamentarians, usually a much quieter group, joined their male colleagues in creating the din. Here everyone was present and the danger was greatest of being suspended from the House for some infringement of the rules.

And it was all theatre.

Despite the diligence of the advisors to ministers and opposition members, the staffers who occupied the front benches of the floor gallery and scribbled notes earnestly to their bosses throughout Question Time, despite a Minister taking twelve minutes to defend the record of a public hospital with more beds for flowers than for patients and despite questions and answers about the state of the economy which said more for their author's grasp of jargon than grasp of finance, the same show was performed each day, often by the same players.

"But nothing ever happens!" Order overheard one of the new female members complain to an older colleague after a particularly heated Question Time.

"What d'you expect? A Minister frothing at the mouth or storming out of the Chamber? Opposition members in hand-to-hand combat with their opponents?"

"Nobody expects Question Time to be informative," the old man, Bob Buchan it might have been, continued, "or to provide answers. It allows individual members to show off their grasp of a portfolio an' - most importantly - it keeps the strategy boffins busy."

Buchan had explained these were the people who prepared the questions and answers, intimating they were zealots and too smart by half. A slight ministerial hesitation in a reply, an obscure issue for which a detailed answer was given, these were moments of significant victory for these staffers.

"But they never get reported."

"Of course not. You need an eagle eye or ear to notice. The media doesn't pick up those nuances. It's only interested in the obvious. Question time entirely devoted to education issues, for example, probably will see a story about the Government being hammered on the crisis in schools, 'though you can't be too sure …"

At that point Buchan and his protégée had moved from earshot and Order recalled another of Bernie's pieces of cautionary advice.

"The most dangerous people in a parliament are not the

opposition and not even your party colleagues, 'though they're a close second. They're your party's own, usually senior, staff. Your so-called minders."

"Don't let them set the agenda, you're the one at the sharp end of the debate, you're the one who can lose your seat. Good servants but bad masters because ultimately, you're responsible not them."

Now he knew Bernie was right, recalling a recent pep talk for backbenchers - training much favoured by Fearless Leader - when some expert had confidently informed his bored listeners most parliamentary performance was tactical not practical.

The memory depressed him so much Order bowed his way from the Chamber in search of a cappuccino.

TWENTY TWO

"**B**etty Downer wants to know what's happening about her fence," Liz reported as he came to collect his papers for House duty.

His desk was littered with telephone slips, only one of which, Monica's asking him to contact her, really interested him.

"Full moon?" he asked Liz through the doorway, surveying all the messages.

"Long weekend."

It was well-known in parliamentary circles a full moon prompted the crazies to contact their elected representatives. A similar phenomenon occurred before public holidays; however its genesis was not loopy behaviour but a simple wish to try to get one's difficulties in order before relaxing.

And because most peoples' difficulties could not be resolved as easily nor as speedily - which they themselves knew - the next and best alternative was to pass on the problem to someone else.

The Christmas and Easter longer public holiday periods were worse for this pass-the-problem game but three day weekends had their share.

"So what do we do?" Order was sufficiently experienced to realise this telephone blitz was a regular occurrence but the number of messages so far ahead of the holiday awed him.

"Let me have them back, I'll deal with them," Liz said diplomatically, "Thought you'd better check them over in case there was anything important."

It was never a good idea to organise anything on nights when the House was sitting; it was an invitation to sit late, usually very late. Yet Order, slouched now on his backbench seat surrounded by the din of Question Time, was determined to see Monica again as soon as possible. Why, she might even have met Wilga in the meantime, he reasoned, trying to excuse his lustful thoughts.

He was third speaker for the Opposition on a Matter of Public Importance initiated by one of the smaller parties from the cross bench.

With only one hour for the debate, it was unlikely he would be called. Nevertheless he had to be ready and sat holding a single sheet listing six brief points while he listened to a Government ex-minister refuting the impassioned arguments put forward by the proposer of the MPI.

Len Duncan was a veteran, retiring at the next election and so old he had earned the nickname Old Len Duncan or OLD for short.

Old or not, he was unmoved by the sanctimonious hectoring of Sean Seymour - or Seeless as his critics dubbed him.

Order had noticed experienced politicians seemed to get stoked up and spoke as if they were, the words inexorably churned out from some inexhaustible supply stored inside them, delivered un-emotionally but relentlessly, yet at the end of the speech you couldn't remember what had been said.

The Opposition's own lead speaker had a tendency to mumble into the microphone so nobody could understand what he was saying. It didn't matter however, because there was no resolution from an MPI, it was just talked out.

Unfortunately this made the device a favourite political tactic of cross bench members, who believed their electoral mandate covered local, national and international responsibilities.

This today-Canberra-tomorrow-the-world attitude irritated

Order. He understood the Government indulged the cross bench in return for their voting support, nevertheless he saw it as a waste of the Parliament's time and recognised the confidence displayed in solving the world's problems was in direct proportion to the distance from and responsibility for the matter under discussion.

No wonder OLD delivered an unremarkable and unimportant response on behalf of the Government.

The afternoon session dragged on into the evening. Order joined Rob Glasson and Tim Forbes for a restaurant pizza after warning an unfazed Monica he would be calling by late.

Although disappointed she was going back to Sydney tomorrow for the weekend, her willingness to see him at any hour while here was cheering and he joked easily with his friends over dinner at the unsuccessful attempts of another member of the Opposition to bed an attractive young staffer.

"Brian reckons it's a pity her hormones aren't as strongly developed as her political philosophy," said Tim.

"He'd still have no chance," was Rob's opinion.

"What gets into blokes like Brian?"

"You seen his wife?"

"Rumour has it he's always willing to join a late debate or speak on the adjournment if it delays him getting home until the kids are in bed."

"How many?"

"Four, I think."

"There you go then."

After dinner the Chamber had a stale air, the lights seemed hotter and the tempers shorter. Those members who had had a few drinks with their meal or perhaps only a few drinks, retired to their offices if they were wise while those on House duty looked aggressive without needing alcoholic stimulant.

This was the dangerous time, when the parliament because of its member's drinks, drugs or plain tiredness often erupted into amazingly petty or obtuse verbal brawls generally involving particular individuals and misinterpretations of what they'd said.

House duty over, Order sat in his empty silent office watching the Chamber through the in-house television with the sound off. Liz had gone home, her contract didn't run to attendance at night sittings, and he was lonely.

He hadn't felt this way for months.

The adrenalin of the campaign and then the by-election win, the bewildering first few weeks of settling into political life, making speeches, attending electorate functions, being flattered and fawned upon, there was no time to be lonely – nor to chase skirt.

Monica had changed this, reminding him he was a forty something man with normal male needs.

But he also was a politician and the dinner conversation about poor desperately philandering Brian had stayed with him. How much more vulnerable was he, a bachelor, to the temptations of the political groupies and worshiping young secretaries around the parliament? Would he end up a similar figure of fun and pity?

A wife was very useful to any politician, whether she helped in the electorate or stayed home looking after young children, like the wives of Rob and Tim.

Wives provided stability, they provided a safe harbour, yes including sex he assumed, and they provided steadfast political loyalty even in divorce so he understood.

It was not much fun being the spouse of a politician. Certainly, you got to go to some interesting events meeting interesting people, but you also had no private life and in public always were in the spotlight.

No daggy clothes or dressing gown for a rush to the shops, no media demonstrations about child care costs, no drinking in bars nor playing poker machines in clubs. In fact, not much at all, save the negative acceptance of long absences by your life partner or significant other.

Indeed, Order had formed the opinion most of his colleagues had no life than this legislature. The young and ambitious, the middle-aged and powerful, and the old and influential: all were wedded to the building and the Chamber for as many hours of each day, each week and each year as was necessary. No wonder so many marriages broke down.

Order had a theory about these divorces and it simply was that most couples married before the political career began and the subsequent adjustments proved too many and too major.

It was a comfort to know Monica would be aware what she was taking on.

TWENTY THREE

"We might as well go together," George Graham decided and Order could not think quickly enough to make up an excuse.

A pleasant enough middle-aged man with a stomach to match, George Graham Order had been warned also was a loose cannon, definitely a maverick, who hated - and that was the word - hated political correctness.

This deep and abiding fanaticism often made him embarrassing to be with as he outspokenly continued his personal crusade against the insidious public blackmailer.

In Canberra such a quest kept him very busy, because there seemed to be a large but anonymous bureaucracy devoted exclusively to creating new euphemisms for old understandings and ruthlessly insisting the new language be used.

George would have none of it, but then he hadn't much time for a lot of other things either.

"Ever notice," he commented, changing lanes to overtake a slower moving car, "that the slowest drivers are Asians?"

They were on their way to a primary school assembly where prizes would be presented for a successful charity drive.

"Don't forget the party meeting," Harold Chambers had warned.

"What did they raise?" George asked.

"Almost three hundred dollars," Order explained, "Not bad for a primary school medieval fair."

"Buggered if I know how they learn anything from these games though."

Order said nothing. He too often wondered why schools held these often time-consuming extra curricula activities, but he was too tired to discuss educational priorities with George Graham. The House had risen at five past eleven and there had been a later night with Monica.

"What's it for?"

"Pardon?"

"What's the money going to?"

"One of the disability groups. It's in the invitation," Order took the folded paper from his pocket.

"No matter. We're only part of rent-a-crowd. Craddock will make the speech. Just make sure he knows we're here."

As Opposition members they had no formal role in the proceedings. Bob Craddock, Education Minister, was doing the honours. Order was there as a member of the Education Committee and George because it was his electorate.

"We should be in time for that."

"Craddock's always late anyway."

Both men were echoing Bernie's advice: you must tell your hosts you're present. If you don't let them know, how can they tell everyone else?

It was particularly important to identify yourself to the political guest-of-honour because it was the only sure way of being acknowledged. Organisers sometimes became flustered and forgot to identify you, however if you could register you were there with your political colleague an unwritten code required them to mention you by name.

Order knew it was the only recognition they'd receive while they were present. Political niceties dictated the opposition's presence was noted then ignored at public functions.

As local dignitaries, seats had been reserved for them at the front of the hall. Because it was his electorate George was stopping and starting, shaking hands and talking the length of the aisle, leaving Order isolated and the little girl usherette very bewildered.

"Don't worry about him, love," Order surprised himself by saying. "You show me where I'm to sit."

The seats were the usual school issue which needed to be individually lowered and in doing so Order saw Gabby Williams sitting in the row behind.

"Granddaughter," Williams said as they shook hands.

Still a small town in many ways, Order thought. A plus usually but it was liberating to get away.

"Am I supposed to tell you if I leave Canberra?" he asked as the policeman was settling back in his seat.

"Overseas trip?"

"No. Just going to the Melville's property near Cooma for lunch on Sunday."

"We can allow it," Williams agreed, as George Graham banged down the seat beside Order.

"Went on a bit too long," George said driving back, "but then the length of a speech usually is determined by the number of constituents listening."

"Listening, George?"

"Well, present. Haven't you noticed the way members perk up when there's a crowd in the public gallery?"

"Not too many today for Craddock."

"Enough. He's under challenge for pre-selection I hear, so anybody who might put in a good word or reports he's hard working is good value."

"So who's the challenger or is it just general dissatisfaction?"

"Can't have one without the other, John," George skillfully negotiated a roundabout in the outside lane, out-manoeuvring the elderly driver on the inside who had the right-of-way. "Various branch members are pissed off with Craddock's right wing factional leanings - he's never really declared himself one way or the other, y'know. So he's now being challenged for pre-selection."

"Anyone we know?"

"Don't even know the name. Kerryn somebody. Typical. Bloody affirmative action again. Got to have a woman, as if we haven't enough already with their bloody soft approach to social issues an' their puritan attitude."

"Howso?"

"You haven't been on an interstate committee visit yet? No, thought not. Once these were good times, the members worked hard, played hard. Now we've more women in parliament an' they feel compelled to be more dedicated to the sisterhood than to any male colleague. Interstate travel on committee business has almost degenerated into vegan meals, mineral water, two star hotels an' early nights."

"No sex," Order teased.

"Oh yeah? Are there any of our affirmative action colleagues you'd want to tumble?"

"So what are Craddock's chances of winning the pre-selection?" Order asked, changing the subject to ward off the unpleasant images George had created of the female politicians in their legislature naked before him.

"Even money at present. He's got a few months before he faces the heat an' I've no doubt he'll be building his support in the branches an' signing up new members."

"Branch stacking?"

"Encouraging people to join the party to strengthen our democratic system, John."

"Craddock's another problem too," George added, pulling onto the slope toward the underground car park.

"Which is?"

"The Micks."

"The mix?" The blend, the diverse hoi polloi, the so-called

multicultural mafia today's elected members now feared, thanks to the unashamed and unnecessary wooing of migrants years earlier by their political predecessors.

"The Catholics, John," George brought the car to a standstill in his parking space. "Are *you* a Mick?"

"No. I'm not really anything. I was brought up an Anglican -"

"Great," George interrupted. "We Protestants have to stick together in parliament. Doesn't matter what party, because issues come up that aren't always conscience votes, like euthanasia, deliberate womb death, stem cell research."

"You're point?" Order now well understood the warnings of others; George Graham was as prejudicial as the people he criticised.

"The number of Catholic members of parliament is a worry. I know by saying this I'm being very politically incorrect, but somebody's got to say it. The increase in Catholics being elected to parliament is of concern, particularly to people like me. They all tend to be socially caring an' like nothing better than to get the government to fund their religious convictions with other people's money - other taxpayers, that is."

"So Craddock's under pre-selection threat by some Catholic woman called Kerryn?"

"You've got it."

"I haven't heard about this around the House, George. You seem very well informed about government-side infighting."

"Should be," As they walked away Graham squeezed his car's security button. "My wife's a member of Craddock's branch."

TWENTY FOUR

Tuesday was a happening day.

Nobody knew why this should be but it occurred regularly. Various diverse groups in Canberra individually decided to have a function of some sort upon the same date.

If this problem of multiple invitations was not enough, often the difficulty of what to accept was compounded by these events also falling upon a sitting day. Perhaps it simply showed the real distain the electorate held for its representatives and their presence at its activities - or so said the cynics.

Whatever the reasons, Order found himself committed to attend a lunchtime rally about a rumoured school closure and in so doing having to refuse a buffet meal where useful contacts could have been made. He was on House duty most of the afternoon, hoped to look in at a Girl Guides' award night during the dinner recess and, if the House rose early enough, a Rotary welcome to new Australian citizens.

Monica would be in for another late visit, although as he hadn't been able to contact her so far today he hoped she was seeing Wilga and would have something to tell him however late it was.

Meantime, he was sitting in his office at the round table and not officiously behind his desk, listening to a constituent's complaint about a parking fine.

"I swear I wasn't over the time, Mr. Order."

"You say you got a ticket from the machine, placed it on the dashboard where it could be seen an' when you came back to your car - within the time limit - you'd been booked. Is that right?"

"Exactly."

"I see by the infringement notice the booking was 1405 hours at Dickson an' you say you had a ticket for 1415?"

"Correct."

"Well, I can't see a problem. All we have to do is send a copy of the ticket to Parking Infringements an' they'll cancel the fine."

"But I don't have it, Mr. Order."

"You don't?"

"I was so upset at the unfairness of being booked, I tore it up."

"So how do you expect to have the fine cancelled without proof?"

"Because I wasn't over time. I'm an honest man. I don't tell lies."

"I don't doubt that for a moment, but you must see the parking people's point of view. They need evidence to support your claim, otherwise everyone would be," Order's voice trailed off as he realised where he was heading, "trying to take advantage of injustices against honest citizens like yourself," he concluded lamely.

"Yes, I am honest an' I voted for you, Mr. Order."

Order fought off rising temper. How many times in his short political career had he heard or read both an expectation of gratitude and an implied threat from those closing words.

"Okay. The only way we can hope to have this fine cancelled is to present a stat dec - statutory declaration - explaining the times were as you said."

"But they were!"

"I'm not doubting you, but we must have something to support your claim in the absence of your parking voucher."

Order was adopting a timeless political ploy which usually worked if people were not telling the truth.

"Ask 'em to put it in writing, John," he remembered Bernie telling him. "Odds are you won't hear from them again if they're lying. For some strange reason people don't like putting it down on paper."

"Well alright," There was doubt already in the constituent's voice. "Will you witness it then?"

"I'd like to, but as I'm the one making the representations to have the fine cancelled, it would be much better to get a third party. How about the person or place you were visiting in Dickson?"

Of course it didn't always work, Order reminded himself after he had shown the man out. If you had a crank with a complaint about some perceived injustice, you were likely to receive ten or twelve pages of detailed argument, often by e-mail. Cranks also liked to revisit their complaint time and again.

"No news on Mrs. Downer's fence, I suppose?" he asked Liz as he departed for Question Time and House duty, a bundle of correspondence in his arms.

Births, deaths and new Australian citizens all written to and enveloped, Order half-listened to the debates, delivered by members who gave an impression that if they talked long enough they would convince all of the Chamber, including themselves.

The vote was another foregone conclusion, nevertheless these members doggedly ploughed on, usually seeking a short extension of time to conclude their speech, which again usually led to the maximum extension of the time granted being taken.

He knew these extensions of speaking time drove the parliamentary Whips to distraction, because they threw out even the wildest guestimate of the overall time limits for debates, often a matter of great importance to ministers with other commitments or an aircraft to board.

Harold Chambers complained regularly about the generous practice at party room meetings and pleaded with agreement to be reached with the Government to deny all extensions.

The Opposition Whip never had a chance.

The majority of backbenchers on either side of the House liked to retain the option of a time extension so when they finally made their Churchillian speech it would be complete and unabridged.

Time extensions also served the purpose of those who used the parliament as a debating chamber rather than as a means of getting things done.

And while there were many groups in the parliament: the doers and the talkers, those who wanted change to the system and those who did not, for example, so many people in the electorate were not represented at all. The legislature had become the preserve of the well-educated, the tertiary graduate, who could belong without much soul-searching to either of the major parties.

The women members were exceptions to this general rule, Order decided, as Julie Davenport bowed to the Speaker as she crossed the Chamber to the Government side and began an animated if whispered conversation with two female backbenchers.

The women formed a third group, known accusingly by some as the sisterhood, who ignored party lines and occasionally caused anxiety among their male colleagues.

Monica easily joined this thought train and he wondered how long she would stay in Canberra once she had seen Wilga.

Order found this an important question, more important now than the original query over her husband's death. If Monica was successful in her quest for a share of the Melville money, would she want to come back to Canberra to enjoy it? And if unsuccessful, would she want to come back to the scene of her defeat?

Order was sure he couldn't maintain a long distance relationship for any length of time, so a great deal depended upon Wilga's answer. Todd's death, his suspicions, the police lack of interest in any other cause than suicide and the gradual but lengthening move away from these dark beginnings now had shifted exclusively to Monica and her simple justice claim for financial recognition as Alan's widow.

Except that a little over a week ago someone in a 4WD had tried to run him off the road and he recalled seeing a similar vehicle in the Melville's driveway when he visited Wilga.

TWENTY FIVE

If Tuesday was busy, Wednesday saw Order middling occupied.
The day began badly with a business breakfast, a function he
disliked with a passion.

The logic of these events baffled him. Why would anyone want
to break the carefully scripted and timed routine of showering,
shaving, eating and then reading the newspaper over coffee while
listening to the radio news?

Instead you rose, carried out ablutions, glanced at the newspaper
and drove through pre-rush hour traffic to arrive somewhere by
seven thirty. Wherever it was always served orange juice, fruit and
in varying degrees of warmth scrambled or poached eggs, bacon
and tomato followed by coffee.

For those unaccustomed to breakfast, no doubt an increasing
number in these liberated times, it probably was a treat. As a toast
and coffee man, Order hated the ritual and its accompanying though
unmentioned myth the guests all were too busy to meet during
normal business hours.

He drove toward the parliament through streets even today less
trafficked as public servants took up accumulated flex time and
departed early for the long weekend, noting two more roadside
memorials and the peculiar habit of schoolgirls at bus stops ignoring
the seats for the concrete slabs outside where they sat cross-legged,
demurely tucking their skirts into their laps.

"Betty Downer's rung again," Liz said as he separated the postal chaff from the straw, "an' can you see Les Preen before party room?"

"Do I have any choice?"

"None that I can think of."

Preen was trouble. A plump volatile man, he loved intrigue. Always first with gossip, he was accused with justification of making most of it. You trod carefully around Les Preen and said as little as possible.

"Thanks for seeing me, John, at such short notice. Not too busy, I hope? I'm not interrupting anything?"

"I've more than enough to do, Les," Order lied. "But what can I do for you?"

"Just a tip," Preen leaned forward, "the Government's set to do a job on you."

"On me? Why? When?"

"Don't know when, probably not today. About some woman." Preen looked expectantly for a reaction.

"A woman? Les, even if I knew what you were talking about - which I don't - I've always understood our private lives were just that, private."

"And they are!" Les looked shocked. "No, this is about money. Demanding money to be precise."

"Demanding money from a woman?"

"Wilga Melville ring a bell?"

"I've met her. Who hasn't?"

"And?"

"And nothing! If you're suggesting I'm putting the wood on Wilga Melville for money - why it's ridiculous. Who's spreading this lie?"

"Look, I just picked up a rumour. I don't know any more than what I've said, but I thought I should warn you nonetheless." Preen looked hurt.

"Okay, Les. No offence an' thanks for letting me know. I appreciate it."

"Yeah, well it's the least I could do," Les Preen mollified, took his leave and Order telephoned Monica.

There was no answer and it was time for the party meeting.

While the strategy suggestions flowed around him, Order tried to put Preen's warning into context.

Monica still hadn't seen Wilga she had told him very late last night and while she'd been less than open in the past, he couldn't see any point in being so over this crucial meeting. And why was Wilga trying to damage his political reputation whether or not she'd seen Monica? Where was Monica anyway?

His exasperation at being unable to contact her - and Harold Chambers was in no mood to give leave of absence on these last days before a recess - lasted through the sitting until the dinner break; a committee meeting claiming his lunch hour. However the Stardust motel room was in darkness when he finally visited.

Much, much later, the House having risen for the day and the danger to himself not raised, just as Preen had predicted, Order spoke with a happy Monica.

"I saw her, John."

"And?"

"She didn't give me a definite answer. Said she wanted to think it over."

"That's promising, I'd say."

"I suppose so."

"Anyway, it means you have to stay here a bit longer, doesn't it?"

"Yes an' that's good for us, isn't it?"

Order assured her it was but his enthusiasm did not obtain an invitation for a visit tonight.

"I'm too tired. Can you call me tomorrow?"

The earlier night caught him out and he overslept, barely arriving on time for the Thursday party meeting.

Nobody would have cared, he decided. There was restlessness among the members and a lack of enthusiasm for the day's parliamentary program. Many of his colleagues, including his friends Glasson and Forbes, were taking their families away for the three day break and couldn't wait to get started.

"Mrs. Melville 'phoned through these directions for Sunday," Liz said handing him a print-out when he returned to his office, "an' the deluge has stopped."

"Pass-the-problem telephone calls," she explained. "We're too close to the long weekend now to do anything so people have stopped ringing up."

"Including Betty Downer?"

"That would be too much to hope for, so no. An' Mrs. Boone wants to know about her request for a larger house."

"So what did you tell them?"

"Too close to the long weekend for anything to happen. Have you Chamber duty?"

Order spent a nervous day. Preen's tip off that the Government using the protection of parliamentary privilege was planning to attack him for demanding money from Wilga Melville remained an active threat.

Fortunately the Opposition had not done too well on the publicity front this week so the Government had no cause to divert attention from their own performance by raising the accusations against him.

Nevertheless he stayed in the Chamber most of the sitting. Question time and the adjournment debate were the two main opportunities for a personal attack; however a suspension of the parliament's daily program also could be called for if the Government's strategists decided the issue was politically worth the effort. It didn't matter either whether or not they were successful in obtaining the suspension; the damage would be done with the media's interest attracted.

It was no solace sitting in the noisy legislature listening to an unexpected and lengthening verbal fire fight, with each extra member adding more fuel to the flames of debate, feeding off the previous speaker's contribution to the political bonfire like children on Cracker Night.

This performance would be repeated if he was accused and while he would welcome his colleagues' support, Order knew ultimately it would be to nobody's benefit.

He drew no comfort either from Bernie's advice that politicians unreasonably fear a damaging public statement because they don't understand you either refute it immediately if you can or you do nothing. In a few days whatever it was is forgotten.

"There'll be nights if you're any use to us John, when you'll go to bed - I won't say to sleep - dreading what the media will do to you the following morning. Politicians have such huge egos they think the population follows their every word and action the way they do themselves. Just remember the newspapers are tomorrow afternoon's recycling, the radio commentary lasts until the next hourly news broadcast and the television is a thirty second story while most viewers are preparing meals or bathing the kids. We suffer from information overload, thank God."

Order was exhausted when the House rose without his concerns being realised.

The euphoria of the reprieve, for it was no more than a tactical stay if the Government believed there were reasonable grounds to attack him, was dashed when he telephoned the Stardust.

"I'm sorry, John, I can't see you tonight. I'm seeing Wilga tomorrow again an' I need to be at my best."

"You always are."

"Mentally, I mean," Monica said with a giggle.

"Tomorrow then?"

"Don't think so. No. Probably Sydney for the weekend. I've so much to do there," Monica dropped her voice, "I'll make it up to both of us, John."

* * *

Order recalled the promise as he drove south along the highway on the quiet Sunday morning. As was usual in the middle of a long weekend there was little traffic.

Before it disappeared into the thickly wooded darker slopes of the Great Dividing Range the land either side of the road was green, with cattle and sheep placidly grazing. Beside the road at irregular intervals lay discarded beer bottles and plastic containers. A snapshot of contemporary rural Australia.

Order was pleased to be out of Canberra, however briefly. The city beautiful became cloying sometimes and he was jaded.

The fact was the doorknocking Bernie insisted upon every weekend was becoming a chore. While polite enough, most people had nothing to tell him and even as they accepted his card for future reference, he could see they were puzzled as to why he'd bothered to call.

Order thus confronted an Australian political paradox: people usually complained they never saw their representatives until before elections, yet if they did call at another time the same constituents could not understand why they did so.

And it was increasingly difficult to gain entry or to make contact. More locked gates and high fences, threatening *Beware of the Dog* and *No Canvassers* deterrent signs, together with being unable to make himself heard above radios, televisions or conversations somewhere in the house no matter how loudly he knocked or pushed on the doorbell. In his personal experience too as he had told Tim Forbes, the police had no chance of reducing home burglaries with so many people leaving front doors unlocked and wide open in these hotter summer months while they lounged around the backyard pool.

Anyway, the intimate face to face contact was going out of fashion, even if it still was the most effective. The younger politicians didn't like it, too labour intensive. They wanted a quicker, slicker process with less direct involvement.

Easier to employ a squad of party volunteers to telephone poll the electorate or gradually build up a data bank on your voters through the distrusted Constituency Concerns.

Although in its infancy The Con, still seen as the tool of the inner leadership group by experienced older backbenchers, had a bad reputation for getting names and prejudices wrong in the quest to personalise what were no more than cheap form letters.

Order said no to the offer of its meagre records in the campaign leading up to his by-election victory and still grinned at the discomfort its supporters must have experienced when Rob Glasson, another opponent, had wickedly sent back to them a Dear Robin letter about the Opposition's backing for a car racing track in Canberra.

Turned out the recipient was Robyn and the woman was strongly against any form of motor racing upon environmental grounds.

"Simple mistake, of course," Glasson had said with a chuckle, "because nobody has surnames anymore. It's an equality thing with no respect for age, sex or common good manners - or haven't you experienced 'phone sales reps?"

Order checked the odometer and began looking for the sign before the very originally named Deep Creek and a turning to the right shortly after crossing its culvert.

TWENTY SIX

After he dutifully shut the main gate he noted the dirt road, recently graded, ran downhill into the Melville's property.

From his vantage point Order could see a house with a wide veranda, several vehicles parked in front and behind the building the dense bush which had flanked him in the near distance for most of the drive from Canberra. Open land stretched to the left and the right but he couldn't see any sheep or cattle.

"John! So pleased you could make it. Had no trouble finding us, I hope?"

Unlike Richard and Terry who came forward with their mother to greet him at the car, Wilga made no concession to rural living. An ample pants suit fitted her out in a way the jeans and red and green bush shirts worn respectively by the two boys would not.

"The directions were perfect, Wilga."

"And on time," Wilga continued, as if the matter of her directions being accurate was a given and not worthy of comment. "We'll have a drink an' then lunch. Gonzo?"

As they passed behind the other vehicles toward the veranda steps Order tried to glimpse the left hand sides of two dusty 4WD's for new or scarred paintwork and a *Baby on Board* sign.

"We got rid of the sheep some years ago," Wilga explained, deftly positioning herself - or so Order thought - between him and the motors, "an' now we have llamas."

"Quite a few properties around here have diversified," added Terry, perhaps distractingly, from his other side. "They acclimatise well, no trouble about cold winters or foxes an' their wool sells."

They moved up the steps and paused outside a dark fly screen section of the building. "We'll have our drinks here and eat inside," Wilga decided. "We had this section of the veranda enclosed so we wouldn't be carried off by the blowflies."

Gonzo appeared from the main house with a tray of VB beer cans just as the door to the screened off section opened.

"You know Monica I think, John."

* * *

Order watched her, sitting diagonally across from him beside Wilga and therefore out of private conversation range, as the table chattered and drank wine while Gonzo laid out the meal on an old high wool classing bench.

"Serve yourself," announced Wilga. "Don't let it get cold. It's a standard Aussie-cooked Sunday roast, John, like we had every week when I was growing up, no matter how hot it was. Except now there's salad as well as the cooked veggies an' something to wash it down with."

"Wilga invited me," Monica forestalled his question when, taking advantage of the self-service arrangement, he homed in upon her like an Exocet missile fuelled by the heat of lust.

"So we could talk further - negotiate I hope," she added. Over the potato salad they were momentarily isolated from the rest of the family.

"And how -"

"Have you enough greens, John?" Terry asked. "Gonzo prepared them especially for today. Garlic involved, I'd guess."

There was no chance to change seats either. Richard and Terry like efficient sheep dogs made sure this young ram resumed his original spot so he couldn't even discretely find out why she hadn't told him she would be here.

He hadn't bothered to ask her what her future plans were after she had told him Thursday night - three days ago - she was staying on in Canberra to follow up on her initial meeting with Wilga then returning to Sydney.

Friday had been difficult, he recalled. A few too many organisations had their social diaries wrong, forgetting the long weekend and its devastating effect upon community support.

Apart from another early and therefore intrusive breakfast meeting, Order had attended a lunch. Both functions were supporting one or another of what often seemed to be a multiplying number of organisations assisting the disabled. In Canberra, at least, all disabled people were automatically and patronisingly assumed to be poor and thus in need of other peoples' charity, irrespective of their original circumstances, financial settlements or their own ability and determination to make their own money.

Constituency issues kept him busy for the remainder of the day, a common occurrence in a parliamentary sitting week when most members put aside electoral matters and concentrated upon keeping their party happy by defending its philosophy in the House.

He'd 'phoned her Friday night on the off chance she'd changed her mind about going back to Sydney but there was no answer and here today, south of Canberra, was the reason.

He hadn't tried to contact her again. He had mapped out his long weekend Saturday and once he had accepted Monica's bed, however late, was not going to be part of it, he put her aside and concentrated upon the responsibilities of the electorate.

"Let me top you up, John," Terry's breath as he reached across with the wine bottle would have taken any new duco off the 4WD's outside.

"Easy Terry. I've got to drive."

"Plenty of coffee to follow an' we've plenty of time to sober up before those New South Wales police shits target us because we're from Canberra."

"We'll have coffee outside," Wilga announced, rising like an empress, her ample pants suit whipping around her as she made her way to the identified site.

"All done?" Terry asked later, setting down his coffee cup. "Good. Then we'll be off. Gonzo?"

The man silently came forward and began distributing weapons to Richard, Terry and to Order.

"Feral pigs, cats, dogs, you name it, John. Always a threat to stock."

"I don't shoot. I've never shot in my life." Order looked at the rifle heavy in his hands.

"Don't worry," Terry said. "Just follow me an' Gonzo. We'll do the hard stuff at the pointy end with the shotguns an' you can be the back-up with Dick in case one of them gets through."

"Anything we need to kill won't be close to us here," Terry explained, "but Gonzo put out baits earlier."

"So why the guns if you have baits?"

"Only to attract them, John. We can't lay down poison; the envirofreaks would go off their soft an' furry brains. We're next to a national park but neither the ferals nor the endangered species, quolls, rock wallabies for example, understand the distinction when it comes to looking for food."

"Get John a hat an' boots, Richard," Wilga commanded. "It'll be warm and rough walking out there."

As Richard moved to a jumble of all-weather gear piled in a corner near the main door, Order realised the man hardly had said a word to him since he arrived.

"Afternoon tea will be four o'clock," Wilga called, as with him fitted out they climbed into a 4WD, one without any sign about a baby Order noted. "Be back by then whether or not you've shot anything."

"Take care," Monica called, to John he hoped.

The trees and the low bush behind the house was not as thick as Order had imagined from the approach road and the vehicle had no difficulty manoeuvring through what he had thought to be impenetrable wild scrubland.

Nevertheless it was a bumpy noisy ride which made conversation difficult.

Nobody seemed keen to talk anyway and Order wondered if this hunting trip had a more sinister purpose than the search for a few pigs or dogs. It was too noisy to ask and no point in doing so now, but he was sure hunting normally took place early morning or late afternoon.

They travelled in silence for fifteen or twenty minutes on no noticeable track that he could see. They were climbing however, and the scrub he thought was becoming denser.

With a final lurch, Gonzo stopped the vehicle.

"Far as we can go," Terry announced from the front seat. "Now we walk."

"How far?"

"About half a kilometre, but we need to be quiet from here on an' we have to spread out." Terry had broken his shotgun and was loading cartridges. Nearby Gonzo was doing the same.

"Gonzo and I will go forward, you give us three minutes then follow but out on the flanks. Dick, you over to the right an' you to the left, John. An' for Christ sake be careful an' don't shoot each other if a feral gets through."

Which was precisely what Order feared would happen if something came crashing through the bush between them and they both fired at it.

"There. It's loaded, cocked an' the safety catch is on," said Terry handing the weapon back to him. "I'd keep it that way while you're walking. Now give us three minutes."

The speed with which the heavily timbered scrub swallowed

Terry and Gonzo did nothing to calm Order's unease this was a foolhardy and dangerous hunt. When Richard waved them forward Order had decided not even an angry wild pig would induce him to fire anywhere but in the air. This act of consideration did not lift his spirits however, because he knew it was not *his* weapon he had the most to fear from.

It was almost silent in the bush where no birds sang. Only the crackling of the undergrowth beneath his feet disturbed the sleepy afternoon. Even Richard's progress could not be heard and Order eerily imagined himself alone.

The shot though muffled by the tall timber and the broken ground was deafening in the quiet and he hoped whatever it was they had aimed at was well and truly dead.

He realised there had been no discussion about what they would do with a kill. Tie it to the stock of a gun and carry it home in triumph, perhaps? Take the tail or the ears as a trophy, leaving the remains to other predators?

The flash of red up front identified Richard, who obviously was well off course, although at least he would not be at risk of firing towards him. And there too was Gonzo - and Order broke into a run across the broken ground.

Terry lay on his back, his chest a bloody mess and his eyes lifeless.

* * *

Wilga was sedated and being looked after by Monica. Much to the annoyance of the New South Wales police, Terry's body had been carried back to the 4WD and returned to the homestead, where the three survivors eventually had given their dispositions to the authorities upon their arrival from Cooma.

There was not much to tell. The shot Order had heard had prompted Gonzo to seek out Terry from whom he had become separated in the thick scrub. Richard arrived shortly afterwards having made better progress through the bush than Order.

It was another tragic hunting accident: Terry must have stumbled, tripped upon a tree root, become entangled in a branch, nobody had bothered to check the scene in detail.

Whatever, the shotgun had discharged in the wrong direction.

It was very late when Order declined Richard's offer of a bed and began the drive back to Canberra.

There was no traffic so the headlights were on high beam; nevertheless he drove carefully, watchful for a kangaroo or a wombat sitting on the road ahead transfixed by the brightness rushing toward it.

The risk of hitting wildlife was not Order's only concern, uneasy about Terry's death.

"He was a member of a rifle club," he explained to Gabby Williams the following day. "Granted, he'd had a few drinks but he was alert enough to warn me and Richard about crossfire."

"An' he and the other fellow both had shotguns?"

"Yes. D'you think you could check with your New South Wales mates?"

"If there was anything, you'd never prove it, John."

There'd been enough time to switch weapons and make sure the fingerprints matched, Order agreed, although he thought the shotgun had been handled by the others too.

"If you would make enquiries, I'd be grateful."

With the public holiday, the accident did not make the press until Tuesday morning and then the details were so limited it only rated a mention in the In Brief column. Not until Wednesday did the news a Melville had died become known in Canberra, even if the report identified a Terry Hagan as the victim of the shooting accident near Cooma.

TWENTY SEVEN

Unlike Alan's pitiful farewell, the Norwood Crematorium was crowded.

Many were businessmen, Order guessed from their attire, numbers of employees and politicians from both sides.

Resplendent in black, including a veil, Wilga was a composed matriarchal figure, Richard and Monica either side of her in the front row, Gonzo immediately behind.

United in grief, he thought, looking at the two women and then wondering why this should be so because Terry meant nothing to Monica.

It was a curiously disconnected service, like most where the celebrant does not know the deceased, and it concluded sadly, the rituals run through with nothing personal to add to them.

Richard took him aside as Order was searching for Monica in the rapidly dispersing crowd of mourners.

"Wilga would like you to come over for a drink later. Say six o'clock?"

He accepted. It was a more private opportunity to pay his respects and he'd been uncomfortable not making contact with what remained of the family in the days since returning to Canberra. Also, he was curious to find out if Monica still was with them because he hadn't heard from her in the intervening days and several telephone calls to the Stardust had gone unanswered and unreturned.

Order wondered too if he could raise the delicate subject with Wilga of the Government's proposed job on him.

Then back at the office Order noticed the chamber pot had been moved.

Gabby Williams awaited him inside.

"Thought I'd pay you a visit, John. Not what you can talk about on the 'phone. You must understand all this is strictly off-the-record?"

Order nodded.

"We've had our suspicions about Todd's death an' your story from Betty Downer added to them," he continued.

"So it was murder?"

"No way will we ever prove it, but there was a motive."

"The Melville empire was - is - quite financially sound, but the loss of Alan's quarter share, to which he was legally entitled, would have seriously weakened it. Something had to be done, we believe, to prevent Todd imperiling what the Melvilles' had worked so long an' hard to establish."

"So who did it?"

"Terry, we think. He seems the more aggressive of the brothers. We've spoken to Betty Downer by the way an' what with the wide-brimmed hat an' sunglasses, the bloke she saw could have been Terry."

Or Richard, Order thought, recalling the flash of red out-of-place ahead of him that afternoon near Cooma. Richard had reached Terry before him, but how *long* before him?

"Terry, who is now dead, Gabby."

"Yeah. Interesting that. An' before we had a chance to have a chat."

"But you wouldn't go killing off two sons just for a business empire?"

"Why not? Anyway, they weren't really sons."

"Different surnames, Todd an' Hagan?"

"Old Melville was a nasty piece of work, by all accounts. A drunk, probably a wife beater, who died mysteriously from a fall down stairs at a previous residence. Wilga's his wife alright, but the boys aren't theirs. They're not even officially adopted an' I suspect are his from previous liaisons years ago."

"So Terry's death means no more to Wilga than Alan Todd's?"

"Exactly. An' it closes off our investigation."

"You know I thought I was the target down there, because I'd promised to give Monica 'til after a talk to Wilga before I told you everything."

"An' now I don't need to be told. Dangerous though John, you weren't to know you were the screen on the hunt. Terry probably thought you were the target."

"Maybe I was lucky."

"Maybe more than you realise," Williams said enigmatically and before Order could ask him to explain the policeman added: "We've kept you out of this an' we'll try to have our New South Wales colleagues do the same. Gonzo and Richard, even just Gonzo, should be enough for the coronial."

"So they walk."

"No charges would stick, John, an' the matter's best left alone. Politically - which should be your concern - nobody's interested. The Melvilles I'm led to believe donated to both government an' opposition parties."

"But we've a murder, maybe two."

"Maybe. I admire your passion for justice, John. It sits well with an ambitious newly elected politician, but ever since Pilate and Christ we've had the law not justice. This one we'll have to leave be."

"Why did Todd have the rifle though?"

"Search me. At a guess I'd say Terry brought it from the Melvilles in the golf bag as you suspected. It was Todd's."

"Maybe Terry made up an excuse to see Todd by offering to buy the rifle - Todd was short of money," Gabby continued. "And maybe

Todd was examining it when you arrived an' brought it with him by accident, then panicked. He was half-cut, you know. When he went back whoever it was also panicked an' decided to get it over with - could even have thought you'd gone."

"Took a chance I'd not see him?"

"Again, you were lucky. He must have been there, otherwise how did Todd have the rifle? An' whoever it was had time to fix the fingerprints when you rushed off to 'phone us."

And if I hadn't, Order thought.

"And get out of the house."

"Through Betty Downer's."

"Nobody saw him arrive," Order said, aware neither of them had mentioned Terry by name since Gabby's original surmise.

"I said you were lucky, John, an' so it seems was he, because as you say we can't find anyone who saw him arrive. Not even Betty Downer an' we've made enquiries around the area as well."

Order was grateful the office was quiet after Gabby Williams departed. As often happened following long weekends the electorate seemed to pause for breath rather than take the extra time to mull over real or imagined grievances. What little constituency business that was transacted during the foreshortened week had slowed to nothing this Friday afternoon.

So Order had time to think and to form a few surprising if tentative conclusions, which still were with him when he rang the doorbell at the Melville's residence.

Wilga herself answered the door and after a perfunctory greeting led him in silence to the rear patio and the bar.

"We seem to have a distressing effect upon you, John," she said, handing him a white wine, her eyes clear. "Two dead, the rest of us wounded."

"My condolences."

"Thank you, but they're not necessary. Neither of them was

mine, y'know. They were business partners," she took a sip of her drink, "with their father's weaknesses."

"They were half-brothers," Wilga volunteered, "but different as chalk an' cheese."

"They grew up apart," she continued, correctly interpreting Order's puzzled expression. "My late husband's idea. Same as his idea of having different names. Whatever his reasons, an' they were probably nasty, they worked too well. Terry an' Alan couldn't stand each other from the first time they met. Monica coming on the scene made a bad situation worse."

"Monica dumped Richard for Alan, according to Terry."

"Yes an' no. Monica was my husband's mistress, John, if the term could be applied of someone who was drunk all his waking hours. Girlfriend or companion is probably more physically accurate. Anyway, after Melville's death she had a brief fling with Richard - who I understand is the bloodline incidentally by a first marriage - then she married Alan. A sort of Melville groupie."

No wonder she believes she's entitled to a share of the estate, Order thought.

"Why are you telling me this?"

"Because there appears to be some misunderstandings between you and the Melville family an' I wanted to set the record straight before we go away."

"You're leaving Canberra? For how long?"

"In a moment. First things first. Alan suicides and you were unfortunately present. Then a chance comment by a silly old woman set you thinking his death was something more. Terry, I know, tried to warn - well threaten - you off, just like his father would have done, while I tried a more civilised an' I hope sensible approach. Then Terry dies in a hunting accident an' I suppose your suspicions increased?"

"Let me assure you, John," she continued, pouring herself another wine, "nothing could be further from the truth. One death was self-inflicted, one accidental, a double tragedy which has forced me to bring forward an expansion program."

"I'm relocating the Melville businesses to Sydney. We've been planning to do so for some time, that's why Terry was located there - to suss out the opportunities. Canberra's become too small an' with all that's happened I'm not sure we're welcome here anymore."

"I shouldn't imagine anyone would feel anything other than deep sympathy for you, Wilga."

"Nice of you to think so but it's not the case. We've a business reputation to maintain an' we don't do much for confidence if half the company gets blown away. Nevertheless, our business standing isn't really the problem, because we could weather this. It's something more intangible called social acceptance. The Melvilles have been fighting for it for years in Canberra. We've done everything, right address, generous charity and, yes, political donations, good employers, all without success an' now these deaths have trashed our chances pretty much for good, I'd say. So I've decided to move on. Somewhere more anonymous, like a big city."

"You'll be missed."

"Bullshit, John. Our money might be, but we won't. Anyway, Richard will be looking after our local interests until we can find a manager, so Canberra can prove me wrong by the way it treats him."

"When d'you leave?"

"Monica's gone already, I'm leaving tomorrow."

"Monica?"

"I thought it only fair, to be kind really, to get her out of Canberra as fast as possible after Terry's funeral."

"What's that got to do with Monica?" Order croaked, sensing he was about to learn something he didn't want to know.

The eyes met his in a defiant triumphant stare.

"Because they were what used to be called an item, John. Both in Sydney after the separation from Alan, perhaps even before, an' certainly here in Canberra." Wilga's expression softened. "You didn't know, did you?"

"I didn't approve. Monica seems to have been a male Melville disease - deadly in some cases - but I couldn't shake Terry's passion."

"I was seeing her too," Order admitted, realising how much the Melvilles' had known as a consequence.

"Again, I didn't approve, but it was Terry's business. Monica's too, of course, an' the way she conducted herself was impressive, even tho' I didn't agree with the two-timing. In fact, I was so reluctantly impressed she's joining me in the Sydney relocation. She's got more balls than any of the boys, believe me."

"An' she's gone already?"

"Yes." Wilga again looked Order in the eyes. "I asked you here to break this news, John, because Monica's not for you, she's not really for anybody. Monica's like me, a calculating type, which is why we're going to work together so well and very successfully."

"Where can I get in touch?"

"You can't. Not if you've any sense. You've a political career ahead, John, an' someone like Monica wouldn't fit. Forget her an' go looking for a more electorally acceptable partner, someone you need for more than a regular bonk."

Wilga turned away and, as if on cue, Gonzo appeared from inside the house.

"Mr. Order is leaving now. Would you please show him out, Gonzo," and turning back, "Goodbye an' good luck, John. No hard feelings, I hope?"

Driving slowly out of the Melville's driveway, so slowly he could hear the scrunch of the pebbles under the tyres, Order remembered being Friday it was late night shopping.

Half an hour later he was loading the boot outside of Magnet Mart in Woden, hoping Mrs. Downer's fence was the standard height so tomorrow the palings he had purchased would fit the gaps without the need to level them off.

And then he'd resume his doorknocking.

www.ingramcontent.com/pod-product-compliance
Lightning Source LLC
Chambersburg PA
CBHW020343260626
47156CB00004B/1664